The Encore Bride

Denise Devine

USA Today Bestselling Author

A Sweet Contemporary Romance About Second Chances

Wild Prairie Rose Books

The Encore Bride

Print Edition

Copyright 2017 by Denise Devine

https://www.deniseannettedevine.com

The Encore Bride is a work of fiction. Names, characters, and incidents depicted in this book are products of the author's imagination or are used fictitiously. Any resemblance to actual events, locales, organizations, or persons, living or dead, is entirely coincidental and beyond the intent of the author or the publisher. No part of this book may be reproduced or transmitted in any form or by any means, electronic or mechanical, including photocopying, recording, or by any information storage and retrieval system, without permission in writing from the publisher.

No ghostwriters or artificial intelligence were used in the creation of this book. This work of fiction is 100% the original work of Denise Devine.

ISBN: 978-1-943124-04-6

Published in the United States of America

Wild Prairie Rose books

L.F. Nies and J. Dalton, Editors

Cover Design by C. Flores Martinez

Print adaptation by Raine English

Let's keep in touch!

Sign up for *Denise's Diary*, my monthly newsletter at:
https://www.deniseannettedevine.com/subscribe.
You'll be the first to know about new releases, sales and special events.

Passionate about sweet romance?

Dear Readers,

I've had the title of this book in my head for at least twenty years. I didn't know what an encore bride was or if there even was such a thing, but I knew someday I would write the story. As soon as I started working on it, I fell in love with the characters. Jenny is a tomboy (like me) and has a soft spot for animals, especially the ones that need a loving touch. Luke is an all-around nice guy with a lot of problems. They're both lonely and alone—just trying to get through each day the best they can. But the instant they meet, their lives are never the same again. I hope you enjoy following their journey as much as I enjoyed writing it.

What is an encore bride?

Any woman who has been previously married.

Dedication Page

To the real Baxter and Bentley

A couple of cool dudes.

Chapter One

Six weeks before the Heather Braxton and Brandon Moore wedding

Jenny Landon hurried through Blue Sky Rescue, searching for the kennel of an ailing Yorkshire terrier. An associate had called her from the private Minneapolis animal shelter where she served as a volunteer, voicing concerns that the dog appeared to be depressed and succumbing to "Broken Heart Syndrome." The female terrier had shut down, refusing to eat or drink as it huddled in its pen, crying for its owner.

She jogged along the row of kennels, tuning out the thunderous clamor of yapping canines ricocheting off the cinderblock walls like the roar of an excited mob. In the center of the row, she found the right kennel and peered through the chain-link door. The toy-sized terrier lay curled up on the cold cement floor next to a worn blanket with its head down and its eyes closed. Her heart skipped a beat. Had the dog gone to sleep...or worse?

She unlocked the door and entered the kennel, hoping the little dog known only as "Shrimp" would respond to her.

What kind of special idiot would name his dog Shrimp? she thought angrily as she set down her purse and dog sling then lowered herself next to the still body of the steel blue and tan terrier. *The same kind who would abandon the poor animal and leave it here to die.*

"Hello there," she said in a soft, gentle voice. "Don't be frightened. I'm not going to hurt you."

The little dog didn't respond.

Jenny drew in a deep breath as her heart caught in her throat. *Am I too late?*

"C'mon, sweet doggie, open your eyes for me," she said then paused, waiting for the dog to react. "I know you're upset because you don't understand why you've been left here and you want to go home. I would, too, if I were you. This place must be scary for a little girl like you." The dog still didn't respond. "Do you want to come home with me, Shrimp?"

At the mention of its name, the dog began to cry. The animal's pitiful howl wrenched Jenny's heart, bringing tears to her eyes, but gave her the confirmation she so desperately needed.

Slowly, she moved her hand along the floor. "What's the matter, baby? Are you upset because you miss your owner?" She stopped, her fingers resting close to Shrimp's black nose. Shrimp opened her dark-rimmed eyes and gave Jenny a wary stare, but didn't move. Jenny took a chance, hoping the dog wouldn't snap or bite, and raised her hand, slowly stroking the long, thick hair between the terrier's ears with her fingertips. Instead of enjoying the interaction, Shrimp began to shiver.

"You're okay," Jenny continued in a soft, soothing voice. She'd worked with her share of homesick pets but had never encountered a case as bad as this. "You're safe with me."

She spent the next ten minutes calming the dog by speaking in a non-threatening manner and stroking the dog's thick, glossy fur.

"Is she coming around?"

The concern in the girl's voice prompted Jenny to look up. Patti Reeves, a friend and fellow volunteer, stood on the other side of the kennel looking in. The teen wore black jeans and a light blue polo shirt bearing the shelter's emblem of a full sun with the words Blue Sky embroidered in red. Her short brown hair curled softly around her oval face.

"She's a little better," Jenny replied. "At least she's not shaking now."

Patti opened the door and stepped inside. "Are you going to take her home?"

Jenny nodded and pulled a package of doggie treats from her pocket. She wanted to take Shrimp straight to her place to introduce the terrier to her other animals and help the dog adjust to yet another new environment, but she'd agreed to meet her sister for lunch—and she was running late—so she and Shrimp would have to take an unwanted detour first.

She sighed, regretting she'd let Heather talk her into attending that bridal show and fashion luncheon. She had nothing in common with brides or weddings. Been there, done that, then her marriage had ended in tragedy. *So much for happily ever after...*

Patti smiled with relief. "I figured you would take Shrimp so I grabbed the paperwork for you." She held up the pages. The paperwork amounted to a short contract and a personality profile for the dog that needed to be filled out within the next five days based on her observation. The shelter staff would summarize the profile and upload it to their website along with Shrimp's photo to attract potential adopters.

Jenny looked up again. "Where did this one come from?"

"We got a batch on death row from one of the kill shelters in Texas."

A "batch" for this shelter typically meant up to twelve dogs. Shrimp had escaped death and ended up at this shelter after Blue Sky Rescue sent a specially equipped van to transport her and her companions from a non-profit organization that rescued and distributed large shipments of animals from kill shelters in other states. No wonder Shrimp had emotional issues! Jenny could only imagine what the poor dog had endured.

Jenny's phone blared as she grabbed a dog treat from the bag and placed it under Shrimp's nose. The dog sniffed it but didn't touch it. "Come on, sweetie, give it a try."

Patti pointed toward the noise coming from Jenny's purse. "Aren't you going to answer that?"

"No," Jenny said, intent on convincing Shrimp to eat. "I'll call the person back."

All Heather wants is to lecture me anyway...

"My shift ends in five minutes." Patti offered the papers to her. "I need you to sign the contract so I can hand it over to Emily on my way out." Emily, the adoption coordinator, had set up a file on Shrimp and would facilitate the adoption process when the time came.

Jenny shoved the personality profile into her black leather purse then grabbed a pen and scribbled her signature on the contract. "Here," she said and shoved the document toward Patti, then thought better of it and snatched it back. "Wait, I need to fix something." She crossed out Shrimp in the 'name' field and wrote "Princess."

Patti took the contract and scanned the change. "Princess, huh? If anyone can convince her to live up to her new name, you certainly can. You have an amazing ability to communicate with animals."

Jenny shrugged. "I guess it's because I know what it's like to hurt so badly that you don't want to go on."

She'd been fostering animals with emotional issues for Blue Sky Rescue for the past two years, ever since her husband's sudden death had left her bereft and alone. Reaching out to pets in need had given her great comfort. Their unconditional love filled the gaping hole in her soul that Adam's passing had created.

"Thanks! Good luck with Princess!" Clutching the contract in her hand, Patti waved goodbye with it and left the kennel.

Jenny turned her attention back to Princess and smiled with relief as the dog tentatively licked the bite-sized treat. Princess, wholly unaware of her new name, suddenly swallowed it whole and looked up, her dark liquid eyes watching Jenny with a sorrowful look.

"Come on, baby, we're going for a ride." Jenny opened the sling, sliding it next to the dog. "Now, don't be afraid," she said soothingly as she picked up the terrier and deposited it inside the thick fabric. Princess began to yelp, prompting her to quickly tuck the dog inside and stand up, lifting the sling at the same time. "See, that didn't hurt, did it?" She slipped the strap over her head to position the dog against her chest, snatched her purse, and left the kennel.

Her phone began to ring again.

"I'm on my way, Heather," she said as she answered the call and pressed the phone against her ear. "I'll be downtown in a few minutes." *Well, maybe a few minutes plus twenty...*

"You were supposed to be here an hour ago! We planned to look at dresses," Heather snapped. "Now I'll have to do it by myself. Really, Jenny, you've known about this event for weeks. Couldn't you have made the effort to be on time?"

Jenny pushed open the shelter's main doors and squinted as she burst into the bright April sun. "I said I'm coming! I had a slight emergency, but I *will* be there in time for the luncheon and the fashion show. I promise!"

Heather made a frustrated *humph* followed by a loud sigh. "You'd better, Jenny. I'm counting on you."

"Okay, okay, see you soon..."

She tossed her phone back into her purse and slipped on a pair of designer sunglasses as her ankle boots crunched on the gravel parking lot. The warm breeze lifted her long, thick hair off her shoulders and swirled it around her face. The beautiful spring day should have elevated her spirits, but the thought of revisiting old wounds dampened her soul like a heavy cloud.

I'd rather go home and clean Jackie Boy's litter box than attend Heather's boring, overpriced dog and pony show.

But she'd promised her sister she'd go so she couldn't back out. Heather had spent seventy-five dollars on her fashion show/luncheon ticket and it would be downright mean to be a *no*-show. Still, the thought of walking through the massive convention center with wall-to-wall wedding planners, dress designers, reception, and honeymoon vendors made her stomach lurch.

Every woman believes a fairytale wedding is the perfect beginning to a lifetime of happiness and treasured memories with the man of her dreams.

She reached her blue Chevy and pulled out her keys, pressing the remote to open the doors.

But dreams don't last...

Jenny jerked open the door and slid into the driver's seat, making room for the sling containing her precious cargo. She tossed her purse onto the passenger seat and shoved the key into the ignition.

One day when you least expect it, everything you take for granted can be taken away from you...

Suddenly, that horrible day flashed through her mind, stealing her breath and stinging her eyes with a rush of tears. The day that Adam left this world he took her happiness—and her heart with him.

***

Jenny stood next to a glass counter of a cake vendor at the "The Ultimate Wedding" show in the Minneapolis Convention Center and stared at her floor map while Princess slept in the fold of her sling, safely tucked out of sight. Frustrated, Jenny turned the letter-sized page this way and that, trying to find her location as she tuned out the noise around her. The polished, baritone voice of Frank Sinatra echoed through the cavernous exhibit hall, crooning a romantic song about dancing "cheek to cheek." Women of all ages, sizes, and shapes filled the venue like a swarm of bees, laughing and chattering as they browsed dozens of galleries, shopping for everything from wedding invitations to honeymoon packages.

"I can't even find my current location, much less the fashion show," she grumbled as she leaned against the counter, taking care not to disturb the multi-tiered trays of pastel-frosted cupcakes displayed for a complimentary tasting. The sugary-sweet aroma filled her nostrils, tempting her to sample one, but she didn't have time. The luncheon started at noon, giving her exactly fifteen minutes to find the venue and join her sister.

She looked up, scanning the area for signage, but couldn't see through the dense crowd. Luckily, a young woman passed wearing a banquet server's uniform of black slacks, a white shirt, and a long black apron.

"Excuse me," Jenny said, walking swiftly toward the woman before she got away. "I'm trying to find the Queen's Court Fashion Show. Can you point it out on this map?"

"I can do better than that. I'll show you," the young woman said in a friendly tone. "Just follow the carpet past the gown gallery." She pointed toward a wide, ruby-colored runner. "Keep going until you see the Venus de Milo fountain. The entrance to the show is just past that point. You can't miss it. Got that?"

"Um...sure." *Not really, but I'll give it a try...* "Thanks."

Jenny headed toward the red runner, repeating the directions under her breath as she came upon the gown gallery, a stunning collection of designer bridal gowns arranged on shapely mannequins in a large circle. The carpet curved to the left and she nervously continued, making her way past make-up artists giving demonstrations, a winery offering sparkling wine samples, a jewelry counter displaying diamond tiaras, and many more. Eventually, she came upon the fountain and looked for the entrance to the fashion show. Just beyond the statue, she saw a sign for the event with a large arrow pointing toward a large tent. Walking swiftly, she made her way toward a wide, arched opening draped with white tulle, miniature yellow roses, and clear mini-lights.

"Excuse me!" A female voice trilled as she sped past the host stand. "Excuse me!"

Breathless, Jenny stopped and turned around.

A short, dark-haired woman wearing oversized tortoiseshell glasses pinned her with a disapproving stare. "May I help you?"

Jenny backtracked to the host stand. "I'm here for the luncheon."

"May I see your ticket, please?"

No can do, lady. Heather has the tickets.

"The reservation is for two under Braxton, *Heather Braxton*," Jenny replied sweetly. She hoped the mere mention of her sister, a popular local celebrity, would convince the woman to let her pass, but instead, the woman pursed her lips, clearly not impressed.

"This event is sold out. I must see your ticket to allow you inside."

"I merely went to the ladies' room," Jenny said, feigning innocence. "I need to get back to my table. The luncheon is about to start and—"

"Your ticket, PLEASE!"

Exasperated, Jenny exhaled a tense breath and moved closer, standing nose-to-nose with the "ticket queen." She had to get into that luncheon and find Heather's table *now*. It was time to resort to Plan B.

If all else fails, act like a diva.

"I've paid a lot of money to attend this event. If my soup gets cold because you've detained me, I'm going to complain!"

Startled by the shrill tones, Princess poked her head out of the sling and looked around. The dog's puppet-like appearance startled the woman, causing her to pull back with a gasp. "Animals *are not allowed* in the dining room," she said with finality as she quickly regained her composure.

"Yeah, well this is a *special needs* dog," Jenny shot back, ready to do some serious sparring. Nobody picked on her pooch and got away with it.

But the woman abruptly changed her tune. "Oh. That's no problem then. We can accommodate your disability or whatever special need you have."

"I'm not the one with a special need." Jenny pointed to the shivering canine. *"It's my dog."*

The woman stared, her mouth gaping as though she couldn't quite grasp the situation.

A small group of women suddenly appeared and ambushed the host stand, talking at once as they fired questions about their gluten-free meal choices.

"Have a nice day!" Jenny tossed over her shoulder and sprinted away while the newcomers kept the woman distracted. She passed under the tulle arch and entered a walled tent in solid white. She hesitated at first, taken in by the sheer opulence of the setting.

The room resembled a small, but elegant, wedding reception. In the back of the room were long banquet tables covered in white Damask tablecloths and low-hanging chandeliers separated by tall vases filled with white roses, peonies, and Phalaenopsis orchids. As she walked into the room, she noted all the tables were set with silver-rimmed china, ornate flatware, and delicate crystal stemware. Between the place settings were more flowers in small vases.

To her left were round tables and to her right were smaller, square tables, all decorated in the same lovely "tablescape." The scene brought back a poignant reminder of the day she and Adam had taken their vows. Their wedding reception had been about the same size.

Bits and pieces flashed through her mind: how happy he looked in his gray tuxedo as he held up a Champagne flute to toast their marriage. His green eyes had danced with merriment every time his gaze met hers. His thick locks of curly auburn hair looked like they could use a good combing, but his tousled bad-boy exterior was one of the things about him she loved the most...

Pushing the image out of her thoughts, Jenny squared her shoulders and swallowed hard to keep from bursting into tears. *This is exactly why I didn't want to come here today and why I won't participate in Heather's wedding. It will bring back too many memories.*

She quickly scanned the room to take her mind off her troubling thoughts. Off to one side, she saw a group of well-dressed ladies admiring the four-tier wedding cake and an ice sculpture of a swan, but her sister wasn't among them.

Where is Heather?

Another group of women clustered around a small table situated near the stage suddenly broke out in laughter. Jenny heard her sister's voice and realized Heather had been in plain sight all along. Heather's career as a local news anchor had turned her into a hometown celebrity, making her the center of attention everywhere she went. Sitting at the table surrounded by ardent followers, she smiled and graciously entertained them in her aqua designer suit and white silk blouse. Her shoulder-length hair looked professionally styled—not a hair out of place; her makeup, as usual, was flawless.

When they were younger, people often mistook them for twins.

She and Heather both were short, petite, blonde, and blue-eyed, but Heather's blonde hair held a strawberry tinge while hers had golden tones.

"Thank you *all* for stopping by. It's been wonderful talking with you. Enjoy the fashion show!" Heather said to her admirers, politely and smoothly dismissing them once she saw Jenny walking toward the table. The women, not affronted in the least, said goodbye and returned to their seats.

How does she do that?

"Well, it's about time," Heather snapped, dropping the celebrity façade as she approached.

"I promised I wouldn't be late for the luncheon." Jenny put her hands on her hips. "Hey, I'm five minutes early."

"And what are you wearing?" Heather made a point of inspecting Jenny's red ankle-length chinos, suede ankle boots, and tailored white blouse.

"What's wrong with what I'm wearing?"

Heather smacked her shiny, mauve lips. "This is a fashion show, not a garage sale."

Jenny resisted the urge to laugh, a typical response to her sister's criticism. When they were kids, she loved to snicker at Heather and make her mad. Nowadays, she kept it to herself.

A tall waiter, looking like a classy penguin in a black and white uniform rushed over to pull out her chair. Once Jenny was seated, he took the folded napkin on her plate and shook it, laying it flat across her lap. "Would you care for a glass of wine, perhaps?"

Jenny smiled but shook her head. "Iced tea will be fine, thank you."

The waiter left and Heather resumed scrutinizing her outfit.

"Where did you get that ugly purse? It's horrible!"

Jenny stared at her lap. "It's not a purse, it's a dog carrier."

Heather's face blanched. Quickly composing herself, she glanced around, presumably to make sure no one had overheard. "A *what...*"

Jenny pulled back the brown fabric and Princess sat up, sniffing the edge of the table.

"I can't believe this. You're embarrassing me!" Heather reached over and tried to shoo the dog back into her carrier, but Princess stayed put, her ears perked. "You and your pound puppies. When will you grow up, Jennifer? You're thirty-three going on thirteen. You know very well you're not supposed to bring that...that hairy *thing* in here."

"Well, I just did," Jenny replied wryly.

The waiter delivered their first course, a cup of shrimp bisque, and tactfully ignored the uninvited guest at their table.

Jenny sipped the tangy soup and changed the subject. "I can't believe you've set your wedding date for the first week of June. That's only six weeks from now. Do you realize how much planning you have to do?"

Heather nodded and took a sip of her cucumber water, letting her soup get cold. "I've got two full-time wedding planners working on it."

"What's the hurry?"

Heather gave her a dreamy smile. "We're in love."

Heather and her fiancé, Brandon Moore, performed the ten o'clock news together on a local television station. The entire Minnesota viewing area knew of their off-camera romance and the gossip columns had been speculating on the wedding date for months. Now that Heather and Brandon had finally announced it, their ratings had blasted through the station's roof.

"My wedding planners had to pull a lot of strings to arrange our engagement dinner at the restaurant we wanted on such short notice." She sighed. "I'm glad we were able to book it, but I have *so* much to do before tomorrow night." Heather's four-carat, heart-shaped diamond sparkled under the glow of the chandelier as she picked up her water glass. "I expect you to be there on time."

Just say it...

"Heather, about the wedding...I really think you should find another bridesmaid."

"Jenny, don't start that again." Heather put down her spoon and pushed her shrimp bisque aside. "You're my only sister and now that Mom and Dad are both gone, all we have is each other," she said softly. "Of course, you're going to be in my wedding. I can't imagine it any other way. And you're not my bridesmaid. You're my maid of honor."

"I just don't think I'm ready yet. I've been having—"

"Oh, for crying out loud," Heather argued. "Yes, you are. You've been through a difficult period, but you're strong." She placed her hand over Jenny's. "You're doing great, Sis. Stay positive." Heather cringed. "And get that dog's tongue out of your soup! That's gross!"

But Jenny merely gave Princess an affectionate pat on the head as she moved the dish away. "No, that's good. Getting her appetite back means she's starting to come out of her depression." Jenny pulled a ribbon from the flower arrangement on the table and used it to gather the long fur on the dog's head into a loose top knot. Then she fed Princess a nugget from her bag of treats.

After that, the conversation steered toward less controversial topics: Heather's latest shopping trip, Heather's house-hunting expeditions, Heather's wedding preparations, and Heather's quest for the perfect honeymoon. Jenny pretended to listen, but kept an eye on the clock on her phone, desperately waiting for the event to end. Thinking of Adam and their wedding had dampened her mood. Though she did her best not to show it, all she wanted was to go home, away from having to smile and act as though her life had not fallen off a cliff.

The fashion show commenced after their waiter served them coffee and dessert. Jenny and Heather oohed and aahed as pencil-thin models strutted around the room, giving everyone a close-up look at the latest trends in designer bridal dresses.

The last model approached their table wearing a strapless gown in ivory silk with a sheer cape and elbow-length gloves. She carried a huge bouquet of blush roses and ivory peonies with a rope of faux pearls wrapped around the stem.

"That bouquet looks heavy," Jenny remarked as the model walked away.

"Heavenly, yes..." Heather replied as she made notes on her program. She looked up. "I almost forgot to tell you, Brandon's best friend, Luke McCarran is going to be the best man. We're seating you next to him at the engagement dinner and I expect you to be on your best behavior."

Oh-oh. He must be a doozy if Heather has to lecture me about him beforehand.

Jenny stared warily at her sister. "Why are you hassling me about being nice to this guy? What's the problem? Is he a dog hater or something?"

Heather gave her a stern look. "He's a widower, like you, and he's also going through a tough time right now."

What was this? Heather and Brandon's idea of Widow Match.com?

"You and Brandon did that on purpose, didn't you?" Jenny grabbed her phone and threw it into her purse. "It's your sneaky way of trying to pair me up with Brandon's best man, isn't it? Well, I'm not falling for it!"

Heather kept her expression neutral. Heaven forbid that any of her adoring viewers would see her create a scene in public, but even so, her soft voice bordered on murderous. "You're being ridiculous, Jenny! It's a coincidence, that's all. We simply thought you and Luke should get to know one another since you both have key positions in the wedding."

"You mean, you thought if you got us together, we'd be so preoccupied with commiserating over our dead spouses that I'd be too distracted to have second thoughts about being in your wedding!"

"That's not true! The two of you have a lot in common. What would be so bad about making friends with Luke?"

Jenny wanted to compare funerals with Luke McCarran about as much as she wanted a colonoscopy. "I know you mean well, Heather, but stop trying to set me up," Jenny said. "I'm not interested in finding another husband. I am *never* getting married again." Sipping her purse over her shoulder, she pushed back her chair and stood. She needed to calm down before she embarrassed her sister more than she already had. "Excuse me. I'm going to the ladies' room."

The model turned her back to the crowd and tossed the bouquet. It flew high into the air.

"Look out!" A chorus of horrified gasps prompted her to look up. She saw it coming down, shooting through the air like a missile, but she didn't have time to move out of the way.

Thunk.

The bouquet hit her in the face and then dropped into her outstretched hands.

Chapter Two

The night before Heather and Brandon's engagement dinner

Luke McCarran turned into his driveway at one o'clock in the morning to find a small mob of grim-faced neighbors gathered on his front lawn.

What did Liam do now?

Exhausted from a long night at work, he gripped the steering wheel and cursed under his breath. His teenage son had recently turned fifteen, but acted more like a "terrible" two-year-old, throwing tantrums, talking back, and rebelling against his authority. His wife's passing a year ago had hit the boy hard, causing Liam to be moody and to act out whenever he became upset. Mara's death had deeply affected Luke as well, making it difficult to deal with Liam's issues amid his own grief. Though he still missed her terribly, Luke had adjusted, taking one day at a time. Liam, however, was a different story entirely.

Luke had barely shut off his Explorer when a familiar squad car pulled up behind him. Its red and blue lights flashed like beacons, broadcasting its arrival to the entire neighborhood. Sweat began to collect on the back of his neck as he threw open his door and scrambled out, anxious to find out why his neighbors and the local cop were on his property *this time.*

The moment he heard it, everything became clear. Liam's three-piece rock band blasted music from inside the detached garage. Someone struck a wrong note on the guitar. The ear-splitting noise made Luke wince.

"What can I do for you, Officer Denton?" he asked politely as the youthful, blond cop approached him, even though the pandemonium in the garage made it painfully obvious why the police had shown up, and why his neighbors were upset.

"Mr. McCarran," the officer fired back, overriding his question. "We've received several complaints about the noise. You need to shut it down. *Now.*"

Luke pulled out his keys and pressed the remote. The wide garage door slowly rolled up, revealing three teenage boys in jeans and Nike hoodies banging away on their instruments. Liam sat on the drums while his best friends, Reid and Ethan, played guitar. They stopped almost immediately, with classic "deer-in-the-headlights" stares as soon as they saw the police car.

Officer Denton walked over to the boys to have a word with them. Luke meant to follow along and observe the conversation but found himself surrounded by several people who made it clear they wanted to have a word with *him*.

"I apologize for the disturbance," Luke said to his neighbors. "I gave Liam permission to practice with his friends in the garage, but he knows he's not supposed to play this late."

"It isn't the first time we've had to put up with this ruckus, Luke, but it had better be the last. It's been going on for hours!" Edith Petrie, a short, wiry lady wearing a flowered housedress and pink sponge rollers in her lavender hair shook her bony finger in his face. "What's the matter with you, leaving Liam home alone? A boy that age needs supervision!"

Several people murmured in agreement.

"If he was my son," Stan Spicer hollered in his Brooklyn accent, "he'd be gettin' a swift lesson with da board of education!" He leaned on his cane and the waistband of his khaki pants hiked practically to his armpits with suspenders. The widow's peak in his slicked gray hair and his dimpled chin reminded Luke that most of the neighbor kids had nicknamed him Grandpa Munster. Luke almost smiled at the thought but quickly sobered. Mind-numbing fatigue from a long and hectic shift at his towing company had clouded his thinking.

Frustrated, he expelled a deep sigh and rubbed the back of his tired, aching neck. "I didn't know until the last minute that I had to work tonight. I've hired someone to take my night shifts so I can be home with Liam, but the guy called in sick today so I had to cover for him. Why didn't you call the shop and leave a message? Someone would have relayed it to me."

"I did, but you never called back," old man Spicer said. "Then I saw dat freeway pileup on the news tonight and I figured you was too busy to stop."

A semi-truck hauling a load of lumber had overturned on Hwy 280 around dusk, spilling its contents across the road and causing a chain reaction of collisions as traffic swerved to avoid the mess. It had taken hours to get the lumber cleaned up and the vehicles hauled away. By the time Luke got back to the shop to finish up, he'd barely had enough energy to drive home, much less check his phone messages and his emails.

"You've all known Liam since he was born," Luke said, embarrassed about the mix-up. "You're like family to us. Why didn't you just march into the garage and pull the plug on his amp? You know I would have supported you on that."

"The door's locked!" Everyone shouted in unison.

"We didn't want to turn this over to the police," another neighbor added. Jim Grady, a tall, willowy man who lived across the street, stood in the crisp, April air wearing only a thin, white T-shirt and worn Levis. "Liam's a good kid at heart, but this phase he's going through with the music..." He reached up and scratched the thinning brown hair on the crown of his head. "Luke, it's getting out of hand."

"I understand, Jim. I would have done the same thing if I'd found myself in your situation," Luke countered and raised his palms in a gesture of peace. "I'll talk to Liam about this right now and you have my word it'll *never* happen again."

The two men shook hands on it as the group broke into friendly chatter, agreeing to drop the complaint.

Officer Denton approached him. "In that case, you're getting off with a warning, but if it *does* happen again, I'm issuing you a citation."

Luke silently breathed a sigh of relief. "Thank you, officer."

He strode into the garage and pulled the plug on Liam's amplifier. "Practice time was over three hours ago, boys. Put your instruments down and go into the house. Pull a couple of pizzas out of the freezer and start the oven. I'm starving." He looked straight at Liam. "As for you..." He paused to rein his anger in check. "You owe our neighbors an apology."

Liam's expression tensed, his mouth rigidly set as he stared at the aging group of mostly retirees standing behind Luke. "I'm sorry. We didn't know we were bothering you."

Reid, a husky lad, gave Luke a sheepish look, his unruly brown hair falling in his eyes. "We didn't do it on purpose. Honest, Mr. M. We just got carried away and didn't realize how fast the time passed."

Ethan, the tall, quiet one with short, rust-colored hair, merely gave a guilty nod and followed Reid into the house.

Officer Denton went back to his car and backed out of the driveway. Likewise, the neighbors quietly broke into smaller groups and began returning to their homes. That left Luke and his sulking son alone in the garage.

"This is the *last* time I'm coming home to find the cops in my driveway, Liam." Luke's voice, though steely calm, held an edge that conveyed his exasperation. "I specifically told you to knock off the music by ten. It's after one in the morning. We're lucky we didn't get a citation! What do you have to say for yourself?"

Liam stood almost as tall as Luke did, with the same broad, muscular shoulders, long arms, and large hands. He had his mother's amber eyes and Luke's wavy, dark hair. The source of his bull-headedness and strong temper, however, remained anybody's guess. When the kid got an attitude, he could sour milk at ten feet with one glare.

Liam stared at him with a defiant look in his eyes, his jaw set. "It's not my fault everyone in this neighborhood is old and senile and goes to bed right after supper. I didn't know they could hear us. We had all the doors shut. Besides, we were *in the zone* and couldn't quit, you know?"

That junk you play sounds more like The Twilight Zone if you ask me...

"That's no excuse. I told you no music after ten and you disobeyed me. The drums are off-limit for a week."

Liam's face and neck flushed with anger. "*Why?* We didn't do anything wrong! So what if we played longer than we should have? I mean, it didn't hurt anybody!"

Luke struggled to stay calm. Losing his temper with Liam never ended well and fatigue made it difficult to keep his irritability under control. "No, it didn't hurt anybody, Liam, but it made the neighbors so mad they called the police. *Again.* I specifically told you to finish up by ten because St. Anthony Village has a noise ordinance, but you didn't listen to me so now there are consequences. No drums for a week and that's final."

Liam threw his drumsticks across the garage and stormed out.

Luke took a deep breath to keep his cool as he watched the sticks hit the wall, leaving dents in the sheetrock before clattering to the floor. For a few moments, he stood in the center of the garage, staring at the floor and wondering if he'd make it through Liam's teenage years without losing his mind.

Or the next twenty-four hours...

He had to leave Liam home again tomorrow night to attend Brandon and Heather's engagement dinner. Given the present situation, he didn't feel like going, but as Brandon's best friend since high school and now his best man, Luke needed to be there.

Brandon Moore's marriage to his co-anchor on the evening news would be a good thing, Luke surmised. Marriage to a diva like Heather Braxton would keep Brandon so busy trying to make her happy that he wouldn't have time to play cupid and pressure Luke into any more blind dates.

Luke didn't want to be fixed up with any date, much less a blind one. He'd buried his heart with Mara—the love of his life—and he had no interest in finding another woman, no matter how much Brandon insisted he shouldn't be alone. Mara's long illness and subsequent passing had been almost impossible to bear. Though she'd been gone for a year now, he still struggled with the unfairness of her death whenever he saw her empty side of the bed. It made him determined never to risk such agonizing pain again even if that meant going it alone.

Exhausted, he shut the overhead door and turned off the light, determined to get through another night without her.

***

Luke arrived at Heather and Brandon's engagement party at seven sharp and went straight to the bar for an ice-cold beer. The private room at Porter's Supper Club had a bar on one end and windows at the other end to gaze at the deep blue waves of Lake Minnetonka while dining on ridiculously expensive steaks, fresh lobster, and other overpriced food. He usually didn't eat at restaurants where he had to wear a suit and tie just to get in the door, but Heather and Brandon were footing the bill for the entire party so he'd worn his best jacket.

He stood at the huge picture window and drank a Michelob as he watched the sun hover in the early evening sky, casting brilliant streaks of gold across the rippling blue water. The lake had a calming effect, something he definitely needed after last night's incident. He'd left Liam at home with the threat of additional grounding if the neighbors heard so much as a peep coming from the garage. It bothered him to be at odds with his son and he planned to return home to spend quality time with Liam as soon as he could slip away.

Someone tapped him on the shoulder. "Drink up, Luke. It's time to take your seat for dinner."

Brandon Moore's sandy-colored hair, blue eyes, and handsome aristocratic features made him one of the most popular newscasters on local television, but tonight he looked uncomfortable in his black, six-thousand-dollar suit from Neiman Marcus. He slipped his finger under his collar to loosen his red silk tie, making his usual impeccable appearance a bit disheveled. Though Brandon wouldn't admit it, his nervous fidgeting made it plain—to Luke, anyway—that he had a major case of the jitters. The thirty-eight-year-old bachelor had enjoyed his independence, but his carefree days were about to come to a screeching halt. According to Brandon, the wedding plans were already in full swing.

"Watch out for Heather's sister, Jenny. She's supposed to be sitting next to you." Brandon looked around, presumably, to make sure no one overheard his next words. "At first glance, she appears to be a gorgeous woman who has her life together, but once you get to know her, you realize she's actually nuttier than a bag of trail mix."

Luke moved closer, keeping the conversation private. "Why? What's her problem?"

"I don't get involved in Heather's issues with her sister," Brandon replied, lowering his voice, "but I do know Jenny went through a tragedy a couple of years ago and hasn't been the same since. Heather keeps insisting that because she's only thirty-three, she'll eventually bounce back." Brandon shrugged. "I haven't seen any evidence of it. She recently came into a fortune from a life insurance policy, so she's set for life, but the money can't solve her problems. The trouble is, she keeps using them as an excuse to back out every time she doesn't want to do something." Brandon snorted. "In the latest episode of her ongoing saga, she's upset with Heather because she's supposedly so stressed out she doesn't want to be in the wedding."

I can certainly relate to that...

Luke finished off the last of his beer. "Thanks for the warning."

He set his empty glass on a tray and went in search of his seat. The servers had pushed the tables together to form a large rectangle in the center of the room. Set with white tablecloths and small clear vases filled with brightly colored flowers, the arrangement looked like a mini-wedding reception. Heather's wedding planners had created a seating chart and placed name cards at each place setting. Luke found his assigned spot and took his seat, noting the decorative menu card underneath his folded napkin.

The servers scurried from guest to guest, pouring flutes of champagne.

Luke glanced at the empty seat next to him and wondered what happened to Heather's sister. Perhaps she'd decided at the last minute to skip the pomp and circumstance and stay home.

I'd rather be munching chips in front of the TV in a pair of old sweats myself, he thought enviously.

Brandon stood up holding his glass. "Attention everybody! I'd like to propose a toast to my beautiful fiancée," he announced proudly and gazed lovingly into the radiant face of Heather Braxton. Brandon and Heather kissed then held their glasses to each other's lips, laughing at the applause from their guests. Luke noticed the bottle of sparkling water in front of her and wondered if anyone else had noticed she wasn't drinking any wine.

Luke cordially touched the rim of his glass with the people sitting on both sides of him then sipped his champagne as Brandon began a toast to his parents. After that, friends and family members of the bride-to-be stood and offered toasts. As the group consumed more wine, the tributes became livelier.

Luke had just started on his salad when Heather's sister arrived. Jenny Landon slipped quietly into her chair, ignoring the festivities as she set her purse under the table and spread her napkin on her lap. She studied the menu card with her head down, clearly trying to blend in so no one would notice her tardiness.

Curious, he pretended to be preoccupied with buttering his roll, while studying her out of the corner of his eye.

Blonde and petite, her features bore a remarkable resemblance to her sister's, but the similarities ended there. Heather's bone-thin frame looked great on camera, but couldn't compare to the healthy, athletic build of her sister. Heather always appeared poised and meticulously groomed, ready to "go live" at any moment, whereas Jenny had a fresh-faced, almost careless air about her. Jenny's golden hair hung long and straight and lightly mussed, as though the wind had whipped it about her shoulders. Instead of formal evening attire, she sat ramrod straight in black slacks and a white lace top. The rigidity of her posture suggested she didn't want to be there. The sharp look in her deep blue eyes boldly stated she didn't care if he knew it.

That one has quite the attitude...

Within moments, a server appeared at her side and filled her water glass. When he asked if she'd like something else to drink, she merely shook her head.

Jenny frowned at the strange-looking greens on her salad plate topped with tomato slices and drizzled with an onion-speckled dressing. "What the heck is this?"

"It's a goat cheese and tomato salad," he heard himself say. He didn't know if she'd directed the question at him or simply thought aloud, but he'd answered before he could stop himself. His fork halted in mid-air as he studied her profile, taking in the delicate curve of her chin and the softness of her long, graceful neck. Through his business, he encountered pretty women every day, but for some reason, he couldn't take his gaze off her.

She rolled her eyes. "What's wrong with ordinary lettuce? Why does Heather always have to pick the weirdest items on the menu?"

"It's actually very good, despite how it looks."

She sounded upset, but he sensed her displeasure had nothing to do with the food. And though he knew better than to get involved in the personal issues of a total stranger, he couldn't help wondering why she looked so unhappy.

Remembering his manners, he extended his hand. "I'm Luke McCarran, by the way. Brandon and I go way back, since high school."

"I'm Jenny Landon," she said and slipped her hand into his.

The moment they touched, he realized he'd made a mistake. The friction of her smooth skin against his rough palm took him by surprise, jolting his senses and scrambling his thoughts. As his fingers curved around hers, he knew he should let go of her hand, but his brain wouldn't cooperate.

She looked up, wide-eyed. "...s-sister to the bride."

They froze, locked into each other's eyes. His jaw dropped as he tried to speak, but he couldn't utter a word. His mind had gone completely blank.

Then he saw the thick, purple, and black stripe underlining her left eye.

Whoa...

His shock must have been obvious because she pulled her hand away and the mask of indifference returned. "It's not what you think," she stated in a challenging tone.

"Hey, I don't think anything. Your life is your business."

She glanced across the table at Heather. "I wish someone would convince my sister of that. I sure can't."

He almost choked on a tomato slice. "*She did that to you?*"

"Are you kidding?" Jenny let out a wry chuckle. "Heather can't open her own wine bottles much less take *me* down."

He had no idea how to respond to her "take me down" remark so he decided to simply keep quiet and concentrate on his funny-looking lettuce.

"I got in the way of a flying bouquet," she said matter-of-factly and reached for a dinner roll.

He snatched up the wire basket and pulled back the cloth liner for her. "Someone hit you in the eye with a bunch of flowers?"

"Not just a bunch." She selected a parmesan-encrusted roll and began to break it apart. "A big honkin' monster of a bouquet studded with crystal hearts the size of lug nuts. It had a rope of pearls wrapped around the stem, making it so wide the model could barely get her hands around it. I saw her toss it into the air, but I didn't notice it coming toward *me* until it was too late to get out of the way." She stuffed a piece of roll in her mouth. "The sucker felt like a bowling ball dropped on my head."

He almost choked again, but this time it took all the strength he could muster to keep a straight face.

"I should never have allowed Heather to talk me into going to that bridal show with her at the convention center, but she's convinced I have to be her maid of honor."

"What's wrong with being the maid of honor?"

She looked boldly into his eyes. "Maybe I don't believe in happy endings."

The sudden flush staining her cheeks gave him the sense she would rather get another shiner than participate in her sister's wedding. Sibling rivalry or jealousy perhaps?

"It's not the first marriage for Heather," Jenny said as if reading his thoughts. "So, what's the point? She paid for a Hollywood production the first time around. You'd think she would simply want to quietly get hitched and get on with her life." She stared intently at her sister sitting at the head table. "Not Heather. She's spending a fortune to roll out the red carpet again."

The more she talked, the more discomfort seeped into her voice and it gave him pause. Jenny's reasons for avoiding the bridal gig amounted to more than a little inconvenience. She held a deep emotional aversion to this wedding.

A server appeared and silently removed their salad plates. Then another server delivered the main course of *filet mignon et crevette*, a steak and shrimp combo.

Luke decided to let the matter drop and get busy slicing into his mouth-watering filet. He'd been salivating over this part of the meal ever since he sat down to eat, and he planned to savor every bite.

"So, what do you do for a living?" Jenny asked in between bites. "Cameraman? Soundman? Are you in the television industry, too?"

"No, I'm not," he replied, cutting off a piece of his luscious steak. "I own an auto repair shop and a towing business. I gather you don't work at the station, either."

"No way," she said, brushing it off with a laugh. "I'm not the type to sit behind a desk. These days I'm a foster mom."

"How many children do you foster?"

"Not children. Dogs."

Say what?

When he didn't respond, she turned to him. "The—the dogs help me cope."

The softness in her voice made him wonder what she'd been through and why she'd turned to animals for comfort. He knew it was rude to ask, but he suddenly had to know. "Why is that?"

"When my husband died, I... sort of went off the deep end. I was angry, I felt like a victim and I took it out on everyone else, especially my family. I wouldn't listen to anybody's advice. Instead, I did just the opposite of what everyone wanted me to do."

He stopped eating and stared at her in amazement. "That's exactly what my son is going through. He lost his mother a year ago and he hasn't come around yet." Luke put down his fork. "Liam seems to be getting worse as time goes on, not better."

Her expression softened. "I imagine it must be difficult for a little boy to lose his mom."

"Actually, he's fifteen," Luke replied, "but it has been a tough transition for him. His mother was only thirty-six when she passed."

"Does he have a dog?"

"No," Luke said, wondering what difference that would make. "His mother had severe allergies to animal hair."

"Dogs love you unconditionally, Luke," she said, her eyes widening in earnest. "Your son needs one to fill the emotional gap in his heart."

He shook his head. "I really don't see how a dog would—"

She placed her hand on his arm. "I'm a volunteer at the Blue Sky Rescue Animal Shelter on Tuesdays and Fridays. I see firsthand the good that adopting a pet does for people. Take it from me, owning a dog will cheer up your son and help take his mind off himself."

"Thanks for the advice," he said, distracted by the softness of her touch. "I'll give it some thought."

When coffee and dessert arrived, Heather and Brandon began opening a small pile of gifts, most of which were "naughty" items. Each time Heather unwrapped another one, the room broke into laughter and hilarious "wedding-night" jokes.

Bored, Luke checked the time on his phone. He'd devoured his curd-filled lemon cake and wanted to leave. He pushed back his chair, intending to quickly say his goodbyes and be on his way when Brandon's booming voice pulled him up short.

"I'd like to make a special toast to Luke McCarran, my best man and a good friend." Brandon stood and walked around the table, stopping between Luke and Jenny. He held up his glass. "Here's to you, old man."

When the laughter died down, Heather pushed back her chair and stood holding up her stemmed water glass. "Now it's the maid of honor's turn!"

Jenny gasped; her face paled, her expression stricken as though Heather had just pronounced her death sentence.

Brandon held up his glass. "Let's make a toast to Jenny Landon, Heather's maid of honor!" His other hand landed lightly on Jenny's shoulder.

"I can't do this," Jenny said, her shaking voice barely a squeak. "I simply can't do this!" She snatched her purse and bolted from the room.

A sudden hush fell upon the group.

Luke stared in shock as he watched Jenny run away, wondering what had just happened.

Chapter Three

The engagement dinner

Jenny shoved open the restaurant door and burst into the cool, night air. She stumbled across the lawn toward a wrought iron bench overlooking the lake, her knees giving way as she collapsed upon it. Her heart was racing so fast that she found it difficult to breathe. Leaning against the armrest for support, she closed her eyes and fought back tears.

She hadn't planned to get upset and make a fool of herself in public, but when Heather announced her as the maid of honor, she knew she couldn't refuse without humiliating her sister and it made her feel trapped. When she saw Heather's disapproving glare, she knew she had to leave. Her sister plainly didn't understand—no one did. She couldn't face the very thing that had brought her so much pain.

"Are you okay?"

The deep, throaty voice of Luke McCarran startled her, jarring her thoughts.

Embarrassed, she sat up and swiped at her tears with the backs of her hands. She didn't feel like talking to anyone right now, especially a man she hardly knew. "Yes, I'm fine...I... I just need a minute."

"Take your time. The party can wait," he said softly.

Closing her eyes again, she pressed her cold palms against her cheeks, hoping it would help to cool the burning heat in her face. "Thank you for your concern, but I'm not going back in there." Her hands shook as she reached into her purse for her keys and a tissue.

He cleared his throat. "I know it's none of my business, but if you want to talk, I'm a good listener."

"Why?" She twisted around. Everyone else had given up on her. Once she had confided in him, would he be any different? "Why do you care?"

The lights from the restaurant cast a silvery shadow across the lean planes of his face. Ebony brows furrowed over dark brown eyes. A slight breeze rustled his thick, black hair. "I care about Brandon and Heather. If you have an issue with participating in this wedding, you need to tell them *now* so Heather can find a replacement. Don't wait until you're lined up at the ceremony, ready to walk down the aisle before you change your mind."

His curt lecture stung. Who did this guy think he was?

"Look, I've already told Heather to find someone else." She grabbed her purse and shakily rose to her feet. "I'm not sure if I'm even going to the ceremony."

She slipped the strap of her purse over her shoulder and turned to walk away, but he grabbed her by the arm and spun her around. "You sound like a spoiled teenager. What's your problem, anyway?"

"Let me go!" She yanked her arm out of his grasp. The swift motion threw her off balance, causing her to stagger. Her purse slipped off her shoulder and plopped on the ground. The keys jangled between her fingers. "My problems are none of your business."

"They are if they concern Brandon." He towered over her. "Actually, I think I know what's eating you."

The top of her head measured level with his chin, but his height didn't intimidate her. She countered with a wry laugh. "Actually, you *don't.*"

"What was it, a one-night stand? Or a secret affair that ended badly?"

It only took her a moment to realize he believed she'd had a fling with Brandon, and it made her face burn hotter. "How dare you suggest I slept with my future brother-in-law! I may be crazy, but I'm not stupid!"

Luke shook his head, clearly not convinced. "Look, Jenny, I'm sorry it didn't work out between you two, but it's over now and you need to let him go." Though his expression softened as he spoke, she couldn't help noticing an odd inflection in his voice, one that sounded suspiciously like pity.

She jammed her keys into the side pocket of her slacks and stared up at him. "Don't patronize me, Luke McCarran. I told you, I didn't sleep with Heather's fiancé. I would never do something that low to my only sister. Besides, if I was looking for a one-night stand or something more involved—which I'm *not*—my type would be the polar opposite of Brandon Moore."

"Then why did you react so strongly to him back in the restaurant?"

She hesitated at first then decided to level with him. She didn't want to discuss her personal issues with this man, but she needed to set him straight. "It had nothing to do with Brandon." She looked away, hating to hear herself say the words... "I had a flashback."

"You...what?"

She thrust out her chin, her jaw set. "You heard me. A flashback."

He looked confused. "Of what?"

Why should I tell him the rest of the story? If I do, he'll simply feel sorry for me, like everyone else does.

But something in his bold, confident manner suggested Luke McCarran wasn't like everyone else. Underneath his tough exterior, she sensed the man had inner strength as deep as a canyon. That strength had somehow given him the ability to carry on after his wife's death and raise his son alone, without becoming angry or bitter.

"I used to be a cop," she said, getting straight to the point. "My husband and I both were cops, once upon a time, before he was killed just doing his job."

Though they stood with their backs to the light, she couldn't mistake the shock on his face. For a moment, neither spoke as she boldly stared at him, waiting for him to process the information.

His eyes quickly softened. "It's been a couple of years, but I remember watching a segment about that in the news. I'm so sorry. It's tough to lose your spouse," he said quietly. "I never thought I'd be widowed and raising my son alone at thirty-eight. I went through the greatest trial of my life watching my wife slip away day by day, but I can't imagine what you must have gone through."

"We were both working the night my husband died." She took a deep breath and squared her shoulders as the words poured out of her. "Adam answered a call about a domestic dispute at a wedding reception. He requested backup, but when I got there, I found him lying on the ground. He'd been shot..."

He grabbed her elbow to steady her. "Are you okay?"

She nodded and swallowed hard, determined to finish her story. "The flashbacks started after the funeral. I went through therapy for PTSD, but my days as a police officer were over. It took a long time to recover and I thought I had everything under control until Heather told me she wanted me to be in her wedding. Then...suddenly...the flashbacks returned. Dealing with it again is beginning to make me wonder if I'll ever get over it."

"Hey, look at me." Luke gripped his hands on her shoulders and turned her so the light from the building shone on her face. "Yes, you will. You've been through an ordeal horrible enough to make *anyone* question his sanity. A personal tragedy of that magnitude takes time to heal."

"Thank you for the encouragement," she said quietly, exhausted from a long and stressful day, "however, it won't change my mind. Believe me, the last thing I want to do is disappoint my sister but, somehow...I have *got* to get out of participating in this wedding." She picked up her purse off the ground. "I'm tired and I'm going home." She paused, remembering her manners. "I appreciate your concern, Luke. It's been nice meeting you. Goodnight."

It probably would have been nicer if we'd met under better circumstances...

Jenny turned and headed for her car, wishing this day had never happened.

***

"You're weird, Dad."

Luke glanced at his son as he drove his Explorer into the parking lot of the Blue Sky Rescue Animal Shelter. "Why do you say that?"

"I wanted a dog more than anything in grade school, but you wouldn't let me have one." Liam frowned. "Now that I'm grown and I don't care anymore, you're trying to push me into it."

Luke selected the first parking spot available and turned into it. "I'm not saying we have to get one today or even from this facility. I just thought we could look around to get an idea of what breed of dog interests us. The final decision on what we get is really up to you."

Liam shoved his phone in his jacket pocket and studied Luke with a wary look. "Why are you being so nice, anyway? I thought you were ticked off at me for getting you in trouble again with the neighbors."

"I am," Luke said, shooting Liam a wry grin. He shifted the

vehicle into Park and pulled out the keys. "Let's go inside and see what this place is all about."

Jenny said she volunteered on Tuesdays. He hadn't stopped thinking about her since they met two nights ago, or what she'd said about Liam needing a dog. After the showdown he and Liam had gotten into yesterday over cleaning that trash pit the kid called his bedroom, Luke decided to give her advice a chance. He had no idea whether getting a dog would change Liam's disposition and make him easier to get along with, or if it would create even more problems, but he'd run out of options.

Besides, he wanted to see her again. He couldn't forget how deeply it concerned him to see her so upset at the party and he wanted to know how she was getting along.

Despite Liam's negativity, the boy walked quickly to the entrance. From the back, his worn jeans and faded army-style jacket gave the tall, broad-shouldered kid an appearance of being much older than his fifteen years. It seemed only yesterday that Liam played with Tonka trucks and wore his favorite Ninja Turtle T-shirt. How had the years slipped away so fast?

The clamor of barking dogs greeted them as they entered the reception area. A freckle-faced teen with short brown hair sat behind the counter. "May I help you?"

"Hello, Patti," Luke said, reading her nametag. "We'd like to take a look at the dogs you have for adoption. Is... ah...Jenny Landon here by any chance?"

Patti's green-eyed gaze traveled from him to Liam, lingering on Liam as the boy leaned against the counter.

"Yes, she is. One moment please." Patti picked up the handset on her telephone console and punched a couple of buttons. "Yeah, hi," she said after a few moments. "There are some people here to adopt a dog." She paused. "No…they asked specifically for you."

Patti hung up the phone. "Jenny will be out in a minute," she said, focusing on Liam. "If you'd like to take a seat..."

Liam didn't move. "My dad can go with this Jenny person." He smiled disarmingly. "I'd rather have *you* show me around."

Patti blushed and began to giggle. "I have receptionist duty this afternoon and I can't leave the phones. Otherwise, I'd *love* to give you a tour."

Luke stood at the counter, drumming his fingers with boredom when the door to the facility opened and Jenny Landon walked through.

Liam's jaw dropped.

Jenny had fixed her blonde hair today in a loose French braid. Wisps of stray hair framed her face, adding a touch of femininity to her tomboyish appearance. She wore the same uniform as Patti—black jeans, tennis shoes, and a light blue polo shirt—but unlike the blushing teen, Jenny conducted herself with an air of authority as she entered the reception area.

When their gazes met, Luke's eyes searched hers, but his friendly smile encountered her startled expression.

"Hello, Luke..."

Clearly, she never expected to see him again, much less run into him here at the shelter.

"I'm Liam," his son blurted before Luke could speak. "Liam McCarran. I came to adopt one of your dogs. Can you help me out?"

Jenny responded to Liam's flirting with an amused smile. She opened the door to the kennels and said, "It would be my pleasure. Right this way."

Patti forgotten, Liam followed Jenny through the main area like one of the shelter puppies, hanging on every word she spoke as she gave him a brief overview of the facility. Dozens of barking dogs echoed throughout the cinderblock building, making conversation a challenge. Every time she looked over her shoulder to speak to them, Luke noticed Liam's grin spread a little wider and his gait became a little jauntier.

Luke marveled at the change in his son's demeanor and wondered if Liam acted like this around the girls at school. His heart skipped a beat. On second thought, maybe he didn't want to know. He had enough teenage issues to deal with for now.

At the end of a row of kennels, Jenny stopped. "What size dog do you prefer?"

"Large," Liam said.

"Small," Luke said at the same time.

She hesitated. "Ok-a-a-a-y, we'll start here and you two can view all of the dogs in this section."

They toured each row, observing dozens of canines and asking questions about the adoption process. At the end of the third row, they came upon a pair of male boxers.

Liam knelt to get a better look at the fawn-colored dogs with white chests, black ears, and black muzzles as they jumped against the chain-link wall of their kennel, wriggling and whining with excitement. "These guys seem really friendly." He looked at Jenny. "Can I go inside the kennel and pet them?"

"Sure," she said, but her voice held a thread of caution. "Just so you know, these dogs are littermates and they have never been separated. We're looking to adopt them together."

To Luke's astonishment and dismay, her answer didn't seem to faze Liam. Armed with this new information, the boy entered the kennel and proceeded to get acquainted with both of the dogs as he talked to them in a soothing manner.

Luke saw the sparkle in Liam's eyes as the boy interacted with the boxers and an uneasy feeling crept over him. He didn't know what they were going to do with one dog, much less two full-grown, large canines. The adoption fee would double, but so would the amount of dog food they consumed and the quantity of doggie piles dropped in the backyard. Someone would have to clean it up regularly, and it sure wouldn't be him. He hoped he could convince Liam to check out a few more dogs, preferably smaller breeds, before making a final decision.

He smiled at Jenny. "They're nice dogs, but I was hoping we could find something a little easier to take care of—like a cocker spaniel or a terrier."

She glanced at Liam sitting in the kennel, laughing while both dogs licked his face. "I think your son has already made up his mind." She turned to him. "Baxter and Bentley are gentle souls and very sociable. They'll make good companions."

Luke sighed and ran his hand through his thick, wavy hair. "Maybe so, but they're a little more than I had bargained for."

"I understand that." She smiled, giving him the impression she'd been through this conversation before. "Boxers are high-energy dogs. They need regular exercise and time to play. Don't worry, I'll check with you in a few days to see how they're doing."

Knowing he only had a few minutes, he turned his back to the kennel to talk to her privately. "How are *you* doing, Jenny?"

"I'm fine," she said, though a note of defensiveness had crept into her voice.

"Have you talked to Heather since Sunday?"

Instead of the friendly response he expected, she folded her arms and confronted him through narrowed eyes. "About what—the wedding? No, I haven't. Look, if you've come by just to hassle me about dropping out, you can leave. Now."

Her accusation threw him off guard. "Hey, I'm sorry." He held up his palms to claim his innocence. "I didn't mean to get you upset. I'm here because you suggested I adopt a dog for my son and I've decided to give it a shot."

The expression darkening her pretty face signaled that she didn't believe him.

"Well...maybe I just wanted to see you again, too, and find out your plans for the game next week." It had been on his mind since Brandon called him yesterday to extend an invitation to him.

Her golden brows furrowed in puzzlement. "What are you talking about? What game?"

"Didn't Heather tell you? The station has reserved a large suite at Target Field and they're hosting a huge get-together. The Twins are playing the Royals that night. Heather and Brandon have secured tickets for everyone in the wedding party—"

She shook her head. "Luke, as far as I'm concerned, I'm not *in* the wedding party anymore."

He didn't know why, but the more she resisted, the more desperate he became to convince her to go. "Yeah, but you're the sister of the bride so that qualifies you to come as her guest."

She responded with a cynical laugh. "Nice try, but I don't think so. Heather's furious with me right now so I obviously haven't been included and I'm not going to invite myself."

Stubbornly rejecting her refusal, he moved closer and placed his hand on her arm. "Then come as my guest."

Her mouth gaped at the suggestion, but she quickly recovered and pulled away. "Are you asking me on a date? We barely know each other!"

He froze.

Am I?

"No," he insisted nervously as sweat collected on the back of his neck. "I just thought...you know...we could..." He shrugged, uncertain why he kept tripping over his tongue. "We could meet there and watch the game as—as friends."

"As friends..." she repeated, looking skeptical. "Why aren't you bringing your son?"

Because I want to watch the game with you...

"I don't bring Liam to events where alcohol is freely served," he said, searching for an excuse, though it just happened to be the truth as well. "Sitting in the stands where the roving vendors hawk bottles of beer is one thing, but attending a private affair where liquor is flowing like water is not the best environment for a teenage boy."

Liam would have more than enough temptation in college; he didn't need exposure to the party scene yet.

Luke heard the squeak of the latch on the kennel door opening behind him and knew he had one last chance to make his case. "Come to the game, Jenny. The weather is supposed to be gorgeous and hopefully, the Twins will win. In any case, it'll be fun to be partying in style."

Liam practically danced out of the kennel, cutting off their conversation. "Where do I sign?" he asked Jenny as she shut the door behind him. The dogs began to whine and anxiously stamp their feet, wanting to follow him. "These guys are great! I'm taking Baxter and Bentley home with me." He turned to Luke. "Okay, Dad? You said I could have any dog I wanted."

Luke looked at the two mutts staring at Liam with adoration and he winced, wondering if he'd live to regret this. Sure, they were good-looking dogs and they exhibited great dispositions, but he worried Liam was getting in over his head.

Twenty minutes and eight-hundred dollars later, they left Blue Sky Rescue as the proud owners of not one, but two rambunctious canines. Jenny escorted them through the reception area, giving Liam advice on feeding and exercising his new pets. When they walked outside, the dogs strained at their leashes, excited to be out in the bright April sunshine.

Luke stood outside the door with Jenny. A warm breeze scattered the wisps of golden hair around her face. Her eyes never looked so blue. "Will I see you at the game?"

She bit her lip. "If Heather invites me, I'll go. If she doesn't, I'll know she's still upset with me for ditching her engagement party and that I'm not welcome."

Luke smiled. "All right, then. I hope to see you there."

He said goodbye and headed for the car. On the way, he pulled out his cell phone and speed-dialed Brandon to get Heather Braxton's number. Heather didn't know it yet, but she was about to forgive and forget. He'd make sure of it.

Chapter Four

Five weeks before the wedding

On the southern edge of downtown Minneapolis, Jenny stood on the sidewalk in front of Heather's condominium complex, doing stretch exercises while she waited for her sister to join her. Princess sat quietly on the sidewalk, nestled comfortably inside her microfiber backpack carrier, watching Jenny's every move. She'd taught Princess to stay in the backpack when the zippered top was open and only hop out if she commanded the dog to come.

Heather had sent her an early morning text, asking if she wanted to meet at the entrance of the building at ten o'clock. They had a standing date every Wednesday morning to run to Loring Park, a small oasis wedged between the edge of downtown and an upper-class neighborhood of condominium complexes and mansion-sized homes. After that, they usually dropped into a local coffee shop to catch up on each other's lives while enjoying lattes and a late breakfast.

After the incident at the engagement party, however, Jenny hadn't expected to hear from her sister. They hadn't talked since then, and she'd taken Heather's silence for anger. If Heather had been upset, she didn't give that impression in her text, but that certainly didn't put Jenny in the clear. Heather probably wanted to lecture her in person.

The wide, glass entrance doors slid open and Heather appeared wearing purple leggings, a matching tank top, and a brown Louis Vuitton backpack.

Her usual sunny disposition looked cloudy today with dark circles underscoring her blue eyes; her fair skin looked dull, shaded with an unnatural pallor. Her usually perfect blonde hair was mussed, as though she had rolled out of bed at the last minute and didn't have time to comb it. But her troubled expression and sagging shoulders gave Jenny the most concern. Had she and Brandon gotten into a major fight? Had they called off the wedding?

"Heather, are you all ri—"

Before she could finish, Heather walked toward Jenny and slid her arms around her. "Jenny, I'm sorry about putting you on the spot at the party—"

"No, it's my fault, Heather. I shouldn't have acted so rudely by leaving before it was over!"

Heather gave her a stern look. "Yes, you were definitely rude, but you're forgiven. Let's forget it, okay?"

Jenny breathed a quick sigh of relief. "Okay!"

It never took much for them to get mad at each other, but thankfully, neither held a grudge for long. After a quick hug and a flurry of laughter, Jenny picked up Princess' backpack and slipped her arms into the straps. Then she and Heather began to speed-walk toward Loring Park.

"I didn't mean to run out on your party," Jenny confessed as they stopped at the traffic light at 12th Street. "I'd had a bad day and I didn't feel well."

"I could tell you weren't yourself." The light changed to green. Heather stepped off the curb. "Is it Adam?"

Jenny entered the crosswalk, keeping in step with Heather. "I've started getting flashbacks again. I keep seeing him on the ground surrounded by men in black tuxedos."

"That's terrible, Jenny. Are you going back to therapy?"

"No, I'm tired of talking about it," Jenny said as she tugged on the brim of her white visor to shield her eyes from the bright morning sun. "Every time I think about starting therapy and taking medications again, the very idea makes me shudder. I don't want to dwell on my past. I just want to get on with my life."

Heather walked briskly, swinging her arms. "Yeah, but Jenny, your life is so dull! You need to get out and have more fun. Hang around with positive people." She stepped over an uneven square on the sidewalk. "The station is having a get-together next week at Target Field and I've got a ticket for you. Why don't you come?" She paused. "Luke will be there."

Jenny shot her sister a sideways glance. "I don't appreciate your matchmaking. I'll find my own dates when the time is right."

Heather countered with a derisive snort. "Yeah, who has time for a man when you have dog poop to scoop?"

Jenny couldn't help laughing, but deep down she knew Heather had a point. She loved volunteering at the shelter. Taking care of the dogs had given her purpose at a time when she needed a reason to get out of bed. One day soon she needed to think about what she wanted to do with the rest of her life, but right now, she found comfort in her present routine. "Luke has already filled me in about the suite at Target Field, but I told him I wouldn't go unless you asked me personally. I didn't want to invite myself."

"Oh? You've talked to Luke?" The unnaturally high note in Heather's voice gave her away. She already knew they'd spoken.

"I saw him at the shelter yesterday," Jenny said in a casual voice, purposely trying to sound like it was no big deal. "He and his son wanted to adopt a pet."

"You *know* you don't need an invitation where I'm concerned. Your presence is mandatory!"

They picked up the tempo at Grant Street and began to run the five-block stretch to Loring Park. They could make the trek in five minutes if they timed the traffic lights just right, but Heather's pace today didn't match her usual speed. Halfway to the park, she doubled over, gasping for breath.

Concerned, Jenny turned around and came back to where Heather stood bent at the waist, supporting herself with her hands on her knees. "Heather, what's wrong?"

"I'm okay, just a little winded," Heather said, waving her arm. "You go on. I'll catch up to you in a minute."

"I'm not going anywhere until I have proof you're all right." Jenny took a hard look at her sister and doubted they should continue. The way Heather stood bent over suggested she'd had a bout of dizziness. "Maybe we should go back. We can stop for breakfast at that little café we passed on the way here. You know, the one that opened last month? We've been meaning to try it anyway. Have you had anything to eat today?"

"Look, I'm fine," Heather snapped. "I just need a minute." She straightened and began to walk again, increasing her momentum with each step until they were running at an easy pace. They made it through the intersections between blocks without having to stop for a single red light. Everything seemed okay until they reached Loring Park.

Heather suddenly veered off the sidewalk, collapsing under a large oak tree.

"Heather!"

Jenny rushed to her sister's side as Heather lay in the grass with her eyes closed, her face ashen. "Heather, can you hear me?"

"Of course, I can," Heather mumbled. "Quit shouting in my ear."

Jenny slipped out of her backpack and propped it against the tree. She pulled a bottle of water from Heather's backpack and unscrewed the cap. "You need some hydration. Here, drink this." Jenny helped her sit up and put the bottle to her lips.

Heather took the bottle with a shaking hand. "Don't worry about me. I'm just out of breath, that's all."

"You're not walking back home," Jenny said and dug into her pocket for her cell phone.

"What are you doing?"

"I'm calling 9-1-1." Jenny swiped the screen to activate the phone. "You need medical attention."

"NO!" With a sudden burst of energy, Heather dropped her water bottle and snatched the phone away from Jenny. "If you do that, it will be all over the news tonight. The last thing I want is for everyone to see my body on a stretcher."

"But Heather," Jenny argued, "you nearly fainted. Something must be wrong."

"I've been a little tired lately." Heather leaned her back against the tree. "So what?"

"*A little?* Those dark circles under your eyes tell a different story."

"Well, okay, I've been tired a lot, but it's normal," Heather admitted, dropping her voice to a whisper. "I'm pregnant."

"Oh my gosh..." Stunned, Jenny stared at Heather's smiling face. It all became clear now. The signs had been there all along; she simply had never connected the dots. "Congratulations!" She hugged her sister. "I'm so happy for you and Brandon!"

Heather, however, didn't appear happy about announcing it to anyone passing by. "Lower your voice! I need to keep this quiet until after the wedding. Do you understand? Otherwise, the gossip columnists in this town are going to have a field day at my expense. It could affect my image and the ratings of the newscast. The best thing for me to do is to maintain my normal schedule, at least for now."

"Why would being pregnant be a negative thing?" Jenny whispered. "You've been engaged for months and you're getting married in about five weeks."

Heather's finely plucked brows knit together with worry. "This isn't the first time I've nearly fainted. I don't want anyone suggesting that a woman in her late thirties is too old to have a baby and a career in broadcasting. The station managers might think they should bring in a younger woman because I can't cut it."

"Oh." Jenny nodded. "I see what you mean."

"No, you don't," Heather said and sniffled as her eyes filled with tears. "This is why I need you to be my maid of honor. What if I become overheated during the ceremony and start to get dizzy? You know me better than anyone else does. I need you next to me when I'm standing in front of the minister. The last thing I want to do is fall in front of everyone at my own wedding!"

Princess stared at Heather and whined, tipping her head to one side. Lifting on her hind legs, the dog placed her front paws on Heather's shoulder and began to lick her chin. It took Heather by surprise, causing her to drop the phone. "What is she doing?" Heather closed her eyes and tried to pull away, but she still had her back against the tree. "Get her off of me! Make her stop that!"

"Princess is very sensitive and it upsets her that you're crying. She's trying to comfort you," Jenny said with a smile as she gently lifted Princess out of her carrier and held the dog in her arms.

Heather stopped squirming and opened her eyes. "Really?" After a moment, she placed her hand on Princess' back and began to stroke the terrier's fur. "My goodness, what a sweet little thing."

She's a sweet little dog who needs a permanent home and you need something to help you chill out.

"She likes you, Heather. Why don't you adopt her?"

Heather toyed with the pink bow on top of the dog's head and sighed loudly. "I don't have time for one more thing. My schedule is too full already."

"You could take her to the station with you every day. She's well-behaved."

Knowing she had to get Heather back home and talk her into resting, Jenny set the dog on Heather's lap and picked up her phone, swiping it once more.

Heather tried to grab it again, but Princess blocked her way. "Jenny, put that down!"

"Don't worry. I'm just pulling up Uber to schedule someone to pick us up. If anyone asks why we're not walking back, we'll say you stepped on a rock and twisted your ankle." Jenny tried to concentrate on making the transaction, but she couldn't ignore her guilt about not wanting to be in the wedding. She couldn't back out now. Not after what Heather had just told her. But could she really set her own issues aside and go through with it?

She didn't have a choice.

***

Luke wandered through the noisy crowd of happy Twins fans in the Skyline Suite at Target Field, searching for Jenny. The pre-game activities were winding down and he didn't want her to miss the start of the game. That is if she showed up.

He walked toward the wide expanse of windows that stretched across the entire length of the room and stared at the open-air field. As he looked past the diamond and across the outfield, he had an impressive view of the skyscrapers outlining the downtown Minneapolis skyline. The fancy private room had its advantages, but it didn't compare to being close to the action.

Heather emerged from the crowd, carrying a bottle of beer, presumably for Brandon since she never drank the stuff.

He stepped into her path. "Have you seen Jenny?"

"She's *always* late." Heather pursed her lips. "Now that she's finally agreed to be my maid of honor, she'd better not be late for the wedding!"

A local celebrity had sung the first few bars of the National Anthem when Luke spotted Jenny rushing in the door. She hesitated, looking overwhelmed by the huge number of people crammed into the room. He elbowed his way through the crowd, determined not to lose her in the mob of revelers milling about.

"Hey, look at you," he said, admiring her official Twins shirt, stretch jeans, and cute ponytail. The top was a flattering V-neck style with gray and white stripes in the front, and solid navy in the back.

"I'm sorry I'm late," she said, breathless. "I decided at the last minute to stop at the clubhouse store to get something to wear before it closed and got stuck at the end of a long line at the checkout." She grinned mischievously. "You can't come to a Twins game and not show off your gear. You have to display your team spirit!"

"Let's have a drink," Luke said, not caring that the crowd had just cheered over the first pitch. Jenny's presence had shifted his priorities. "How about a glass of wine?"

They inched their way to the bar, watching the game on the numerous televisions lining the walls. Luke ordered a glass of cabernet for Jenny and a beer for himself. Maneuvering through the crowd, they made their way to the windows to watch the game. Most of the private outdoor seating reserved for the station's guests had already been taken.

"I've never been to this stadium before," Jenny confessed as they stood at the window watching the game and enjoying their drinks. "I went to games at the old Metrodome, but I guess in the last few years I've lost track of things."

Luke watched the Twins pitcher strike out the player at bat and sipped his beer, wondering why simple pleasures like watching a live baseball game had slipped away from him, too.

Jenny leaned her forehead against the plate glass as she stared down at the field. "It isn't the same up here, is it? I mean, looking through this window is almost like watching the game on a giant television screen."

Luke's hand stilled, holding his long-necked bottle in mid-air. "Are you saying you'd rather watch from the stands?"

She looked at him innocently. "Wouldn't you?"

He set his beer bottle on the nearest table along with her glass of wine and grabbed her hand. "Baby, you're on. Come on."

"Yeah, but Luke," Jenny protested with a laugh as he pulled her through the crowd, "we don't have reserved seats down in the stands."

"We'll find some!"

Ten minutes later, they walked into the seating area past first base. Pandemonium broke out as one of the Twins' players hit a home run. Thousands of people sprang from their seats, dancing, shouting, and screaming to the ear-splitting music streaming through the mega loudspeakers. Roving vendors clad in bright yellow shirts wandered the aisles, hawking everything from hot dogs and pizza to peanuts and beer. The breezy spring air held a tangible buzz of electricity and anticipation.

Luke spied a pair of aisle seats close to the field and pointed them out. "How about those?" he shouted through the deafening roar of the crowd.

Jenny stared at him wide-eyed. "What if the people who hold tickets for them show up?"

He pulled his sunglasses from his shirt pocket and slipped them on. "We'll find some more!"

After a couple of innings, however, no one had shown up to claim them. Luke and Jenny munched on hot dogs and drank sodas, caught up in the excitement of a close game. They jumped to their feet and cheered when a player stole a base or hit a home run, groaned, and complained when the Royals scored.

Luke hadn't experienced such a carefree afternoon in a long time—so long in fact, he'd nearly forgotten what it was like to let go of his problems and simply enjoy himself. It warmed his heart to see the sparkle in Jenny's eyes and hear her light-hearted laughter, making him so glad they'd come down to this section—even if they were occupying stolen seats. That made it even more exciting.

The young men sitting in the seats behind them kept a running commentary going as they drank beer and cursed the umpires. As each inning progressed, they became drunker, louder, and more entertaining than the game.

During the middle of the sixth inning, the "Kiss Cam," a diamond-shaped camera, appeared on the gigantic center-field scoreboard as a love song blasted from the ballpark's loudspeakers. Luke watched, mesmerized as the camera centered on one couple after another, showing the surprised looks on their faces before they came together and smooched. The amusement on his face turned to shock, however, when his and Jenny's faces suddenly appeared on the screen. At first, they sat like statues, stunned to see themselves on the big screen. His heart slammed in his chest. He wanted to kiss her. Would she object if he did? After all, they were only friends...

The burly, bearded young man directly behind them stood up.

"Come on, you guys. Let's get some action going!" Before Luke could stop him, the man put his big hands on the backs of their heads and slammed their faces together.

***

It happened so fast that Jenny didn't have time to catch her breath, much less object. One moment she saw the color drain from her face on the jumbo screen for all to see, the next moment she found herself lip-locked with Luke McCarran.

The crowd exploded with cheering and applause at the quick thinking of their fellow Twins fan in the row behind them. No one knew that Luke and Jenny had never kissed before, that they were only friends.

She had to admit, though, that none of her friends had ever kissed her *like that.*

As their mouths pressed together, her thoughts went into a tailspin at the notion of sharing such an intimate moment with Luke in front of approximately thirty-five thousand screaming people. At first, Luke seemed as amazed as she was, kissing her tentatively with gentle, yet firm pressure, giving her the sense that he was waiting for her to pull free. Ironically, she didn't care when the instigator behind them took his hands away and the roar of the crowd indicated the camera had landed on someone else. Her entire world had focused solely and completely on the man who held her attention captive. Everything else faded away as her palms slid over Luke's broad shoulders, absorbing the strength of his taut muscles, and the warmth of his body through the thin fabric of his polo shirt. He circled his arms around her waist and pulled her close. They deepened the kiss, holding on tighter, breathing faster—

"Excuse me!"

The caustic voice shouted next to her ear. It took Jenny a moment to pull her thoughts together, but she came straight back to reality when the sharp edge of a cardboard tray jammed into her ribs. She jerked upright, pulling out of Luke's arms as she turned to find an elderly couple glaring at her. They wanted to return to their seats that, unfortunately, were situated in the middle of the row. She and Luke stood, allowing the stooped, slow-moving seniors to pass.

When they sat down again, Jenny knew the situation between her and Luke had forever changed. They could never go back to being *just* friends, but she didn't know where their relationship stood. Not knowing how he felt put her half of their friendship in an awkward position. Did he kiss her out of curiosity or because he'd had his face flattened against hers by an obnoxious drunk? She occupied herself by straightening her clothes and tucking her purse under her seat as she mulled it over, but her nervous busyness ceased when Luke's fingers gently took her hand.

His dark eyes crinkled. "That was hilarious. I wonder if we can buy the video."

His genuineness put her at ease and she burst out laughing. "Now everyone in the suite knows where we went."

Luke stretched his arm along the back of her seat, her heart skipping a beat as his lips brushed her ear. "Frankly, I don't want to go back up there, do you?" He gazed into her eyes. "I'm happy to stay right here and have you all to myself until the end of the game."

"I probably have a dozen texts from Heather on my phone by now, wanting to know where we are," she said as she held up her hands to feign ignorance, "but who can hear the phone with all this noise?"

They stayed in the stands until the end of the game and cheered when the Twins won. Nighttime had fallen and huge floodlights shone brightly across the ballpark. After the stands began to clear, they joined the sea of people painstakingly making their way to the exit. Luke walked Jenny to the parking ramp to pick up her car.

"Thanks for going out of your way for me," Jenny said as she fished her keys out of her purse and unlocked her car. All around them, car doors slammed and engines roared under the bright lights of the huge facility.

Luke opened the door for her and stood with his hand resting along the top of it. "I wanted to make sure you were safe."

Jenny paused before sliding into the driver's seat. "I had a great time today, Luke. It's been a long time since I've enjoyed myself so much. Thank you for encouraging me to come."

He leaned into the car and kissed her lightly on the lips. "I'm glad you did." Tugging lightly on a lock of stray hair, he said, "May I call you?"

She smiled. "I'd be disappointed if you didn't."

His kiss stayed on her mind all the way home.

Chapter Five

Four weeks before the wedding

Between Liam, the dogs, and his best employee going on vacation, Luke had a frantic week. Liam had a ball game or practice every night after school which meant Luke needed to make it home by three o'clock to let the dogs out to run and relieve themselves.

Luke's days were booked solid, but he made time every night while walking Baxter and Bentley to call Jenny. He looked forward to hearing her voice, talking about her day, and making plans to see her again on the weekend. He had something he wanted to talk to her about, but not over the phone.

On Friday afternoon, he'd just finished showering and changing into jeans and a gray T-shirt when the doorbell rang. Curious, he walked to the front door, still rubbing his hair dry with a towel. No one ever came to his house except the Girl Scouts and the local cops, and since the cookie season had passed, he wondered what troublesome situation Liam had gotten himself into this time. Whatever Liam had done, the police presence would have alerted all of their neighbors that the boy had acted up again.

Preparing for the worst, Luke jerked open the door and almost dropped the bunched-up towel in his fist. Jenny stood before him wearing a pink knit shirt, white Capri pants, and white sandals. Her golden hair fell past her shoulders like long strands of silk.

Her sunny smile turned into pink-cheeked embarrassment at his disheveled appearance. "I'm sorry, Luke if I took you by surprise. Is this a bad time to drop by? I should have called first to make sure Liam was available. I didn't mean to intrude."

"Oh, you surprised me all right, but don't feel bad about that," Luke said with a chuckle of relief. He stood to one side, motioning to her to enter the living room. "You're ten times better than what I had expected. Come on in."

She walked into the house and glanced around, as though expecting a father-and-son bachelor pad to have the walls papered with Sports Illustrated swimsuit models, or worse... "What do you mean?"

"Let's just say I'm glad it didn't have anything negative to do with Liam for once. He's at ball practice, by the way." He shut the door behind her. "Have a seat. Would you like a Coke?"

The thundering of paws on the basement stairs interrupted her answer. Baxter and Bentley raced into the living room and began to bounce around Jenny, sniffing her clothes and wiggling their short tails.

"Hey, where did you two come from?" Jenny smiled and stood as they checked her out. "You sounded like a herd of buffalo charging through the house."

"They sleep downstairs on Liam's bed when he's at school," Luke said and snapped his fingers. "Baxter, Bentley, come!" The boxers reluctantly left Jenny and came to Luke. He snapped his fingers again. "Sit!" Both of them sat, looking confused at not being able to inspect their visitor. "They must have had obedience training. Liam discovered that they understand a lot of commands."

"They're actually the reason I'm here. I told you when you adopted them that I would check on them to see how they were getting along." She looked at Luke. "I'm glad they're adjusting."

He patted Baxter on the head. "They've taken over the house. Liam and I are the ones who've had to adjust."

Luke went into the kitchen to retrieve a couple of cans of Coke. When he returned, he found both dogs on the sofa with Jenny, one on each side, their chins possessively resting on her lap.

She laughed. "They like me."

He ordered them off the furniture and commanded them to sit again. "Let's go outside so we can talk in peace."

The moment he opened the front door, however, Baxter ran into the closet and came out holding his red leash. Bentley grabbed one end of it and they began to play tug of war.

"See what I mean about these two?"

Jenny set down her Coke and gently took the leash from the dog. "One for you, one for me," she said, picking up the other leash from the closet floor. "We can talk as we walk."

They snapped the leashes on the dogs' collars and left the house.

"Where are we going?" Jenny asked as Bentley pulled her down the driveway.

"Around the block. Hook a right turn at the end of the driveway." Luke frowned, peeved at how the dogs were getting all of her attention.

"What did your son say about our episode on the Kiss Cam?" she asked as they reached the sidewalk, strolling side-by-side.

Luke took a swig of his Coke to keep himself from shuddering at the thought. "Nothing. As far as I can tell, he doesn't know about it. Yet."

"That's odd." She sounded amused. "I assumed he'd seen it by now because it's all over the internet. Didn't he see it on Facebook?"

Luke stared up at the cloudless blue sky, thanking his lucky stars even though he couldn't see them in the daylight. "Liam isn't on

Facebook." He steered Baxter around the corner. "He hangs out with his friends on Snapchat. Is that where you saw it? On Facebook?"

"Yes, and the expression on our faces when the guy smashes our heads together is why it's traveling across social media at light speed." She looped the leash around her wrist and pulled her phone from her pocket with her other hand. After a bit of maneuvering on the screen with her thumb, she showed him the video.

Dismayed, he muttered a couple of expletives before he realized what he was saying. He looked up, embarrassed, but saw only an amused expression on her face. Suddenly, they both burst out laughing.

He walked along with her for a few minutes, simply enjoying her company.

"I have to work late tomorrow night," Luke suddenly confessed. "I know we had planned to have dinner together, but I can't guarantee what time I'll get off."

"What about Sunday night?" She sounded hopeful.

"I have an idea." He cut her a sideways glance, anxious to gauge her reaction. "How'd you like to come over on Sunday afternoon for a barbecue?"

"Sure," she said enthusiastically. "I'll bring a salad. Will Liam be there, too?"

"Yes, he will. I'd like for you and my son to get to know each other better." He stopped and faced her. *Might as well get right to the point.* "I don't want to impose on you, so feel free to tell me if I'm out of line, but I need your help with something that concerns him."

"I'll help in any way I can. What is it," she asked curiously.

Just thinking about it made his neck and shoulders stiffen with tension. "I have to throw a bachelor party for Brandon." Luke let out a deep breath and tried to rub out the kink in his neck. "There's no way

I'm leaving my son home alone that night without supervision. My neighbors are on the verge of mutiny as it is. I'd ask my parents, but they're going to be on a cruise with some friends. Would you mind hanging out with him for a few hours?"

Her eyes widened. "You mean, like, babysit? Isn't he a little old for that?"

They turned at the last corner and headed back to Luke's house.

"I need to make sure he doesn't get into trouble and given your background as a cop, I'm confident you can handle him."

She raised her brows. "I'm sure he's going to *love* that—having a former cop breathing down his neck."

Luke snorted. "I don't care. I'm desperate."

"You must be." She grinned. "Okay, I'll do it."

He did a double-take. "You will? Great! That just took a load off my mind."

They stopped next to Jenny's blue Chevy and relaxed, leaning against the car. The leashes went slack as the dogs busied themselves sniffing the tires.

Luke slid his arm around her waist. "Thank you, Jenny. You're terrific. I owe you for this." He bent his head and kissed her lightly. It seemed as natural as breathing. He kissed her again, tasting the sweetness of her lips. His heart stirred. Suddenly, his arms were around her, pulling her close, his mouth closing over hers.

Across the street, a screen door banged. And then another. And then another.

"It's about darn time, McCarran!" Jim Grady hollered from his front porch.

"Woo-hoo, will ya look at dat!" Stan Spicer's Brooklyn accent sounded loud and clear. "We got us a happy ending!"

Luke looked up to see all of his neighbors applauding. To him, it was just the beginning...

**

As Jenny suspected, the barbeque on Sunday proved to be no picnic once Liam learned of their plans for the night of Brandon's bachelor party.

He sat at the patio table on the back deck, glowering at her and Luke. "I don't need no stupid babysitter. Especially an ex-cop."

Luke's face flushed, his jaw tightened with anger as he gripped his hands on the sides of his deck chair. "Watch your mouth, mister—"

Jenny placed her hand on Luke's arm to calm him. She'd had experience working with youth during her career as a police officer and she knew how to tackle this issue.

"I understand how you feel, Liam and I agree. I'm not your babysitter. That's an insult to someone your age. I'm just going to hang out with you until your dad comes home and then we're all going out to breakfast."

Liam huffed with disgust. "Babysit—hang out, what's the difference?"

"The difference is that I'm not going to tell you what to do. If you don't want to remain at the house with me, I'm not going to force you to stay."

Luke stared at her as though she'd lost her mind.

She kept her voice even. "I'm simply going to trust that you'll do the right thing."

"Why should I?" Liam scowled at the bare steak bone and a small mound of leftover potato salad on his plate. "Why should I care what you think?"

Luke went rigid, the taut line of his jaw indicating he had all he could do to keep his temper from blowing apart. She squeezed his arm, encouraging him to remain calm.

"I understand you've had a few incidents with your local precinct for curfew and noise issues. If any of the neighbors call and complain, they'll patrol this block all night. You don't want any more trouble with them, do you?"

Liam looked up, defiant. "What if I don't stick around? You said I can leave if I want."

"Yes, I said that, but I don't want you to go. Liam, give me a chance."

Jenny sensed she'd gain more cooperation from Liam without his father present. She stood and grabbed the plates, pretending to clear the table. Luke quickly rose and took the plates from her.

"I'll do this," he said and piled up the dirty dishes. "Anyone feel like a root beer float?"

"Sure," Jenny said, knowing it would keep him in the kitchen longer. She looked at Liam. "How about you?"

The boy shrugged.

Luke shot her a frustrated look and went into the house, leaving her alone with his son.

"So, are you and my dad, like, *together*?" Liam blurted, wasting no time getting to the point.

Jenny folded her hands on the table. "Luke and I are friends."

His skeptical expression indicated he didn't believe it. "That's not what I heard." When she didn't respond, he continued. "Grandpa Munster said he saw you guys goin' at it in broad daylight."

Grandpa...who?

"It wasn't like that." Jenny struggled to keep a straight face and failed. She pressed her fingers upon her lips to keep from giggling, but a high-pitched sound escaped from her throat. Once she heard herself laugh, she couldn't stop. "Is that the old man who wears his pants practically up to his chin?" She coughed, wiping the tears from her eyes. "What did you call him?"

"Grandpa Munster," Liam said, breaking into a grin. "His name is Stan Spicer, but all my friends and I call him that because with his hair slicked back, he looks like a vampire. That funny accent he has makes him sound like one, too."

Jenny could barely speak, she laughed so hard. "Does he bite people, too?"

Liam started to laugh. "No, he doesn't have many teeth, but he spies on us. A lot." He leaned forward as if to speak confidentially. "My friend, Ethan, says old man Spicer is a peeping Tom. He's seen the old guy poking around Mrs. Petrie's bedroom window."

Jenny rested her chin on one hand. "Maybe he's just nosy. Do you think he'll spy on us?"

"I don't know..." Liam said as he stared at her, his eyes widening. "I think it would be a blast to catch him in the process, though, don't you?"

Jenny waved her hand. "Let him look. We'll be too busy having fun to notice, anyway."

Liam began to roar. "Maybe we should call the cops on *him*!"

The kitchen door opened and Luke stepped out holding a tall fountain glass in each hand. He stared at Liam's back, looking baffled by the change in the mood of everyone around the table.

"So," Liam said, openly flirting with her, "what time are you coming over?"

Chapter Six

Two weeks before the wedding

For the next two weeks, Jenny and Luke met every day after work to walk the dogs, eat dinner, and simply be together. He looked forward to seeing her and made sure he left the shop with plenty of time to let the dogs out, take a shower, and meet Jenny by four. He didn't know exactly when it happened, but she'd become an essential part of his life.

One day, while sitting with her on a bench at the dog park, Luke noticed Jenny looking downcast. He moved close and lifted her chin to look into her eyes. "What's wrong?" Her usual upbeat, energetic disposition appeared to have lost its luster.

"I'm worried about getting through the wedding. I promised Heather I'd be her maid of honor, but the reception will be tough. Every time I see someone in a tux walking around with a drink in his hand, it will remind me of the night Adam was killed." She looked away and cleared her throat, letting him know she didn't want him to see the tears in her eyes.

Luke slid his arm around her. "Are you worried about having a flashback?"

"Yes...no..." She closed her eyes. "I don't know. Strangely enough, I haven't had any since the day we met at the Twins game, but

I'm so tired of the threat lurking in the back of my mind all the time I just don't want to think about it anymore."

He pulled her close. "Jenny, you need to face your fear."

She glared at him. "You don't know what you're talking about, Luke. I face it every day."

The irritable edge in her voice surprised him. He'd never seen her like this before. "I understand that, Jenny, and I don't mean to sound like a therapist, but the longer you put it off, the longer it's going to hang over your life like a dark cloud."

Bentley came up to her and placed his head in her lap, looking up at her with sad eyes.

She stroked the top of his head. "What do you suggest I do?"

"That has to come from you, Jenny." He held her gently, trying to assure her his words came straight from his heart. "It won't work any other way."

She sat with her head on his shoulder for a few moments, as if deep in thought. "If I need to face my fear then I think I should go back to the scene of the crime." She sat up and pushed herself off the bench. "I need to see it again."

Luke stared up at her in surprise. "Are you sure? It could backfire and leave you traumatized all over again."

She exhaled a deep sigh. "That's the chance I have to take. Will you drive me there?"

He stood up. "If that's what you want, then let's go."

They walked the dogs back to the house, locked up, and left in Luke's Explorer to visit the scene of Adam Landon's murder. When Jenny told him the venue, he grimaced, remembering the details of the incident. The Palisade Ballroom, located in a crime-ridden neighborhood, had a reputation for violence and multiple police calls on the weekends. Thankfully, they were going to the place during business hours on a weekday. He figured they'd probably find the place closed and deserted. He *hoped* they would anyway.

Jenny remained silent on the trip across town. She sat with her back to him, staring out the passenger window while Luke wondered if her silence meant she couldn't make up her mind about going through with the visit or not. Only time would tell what she ultimately decided.

They arrived at the Palisade Ballroom forty-five minutes later. The old brick structure sat on a hill between two warehouses and across the street from an empty lot filled with scrubby trees. Luke pulled up to the back of the building and shut off the vehicle. He sat there, quietly waiting until Jenny spoke.

"Adam was shot right there." She pointed to a patchy piece of lawn, covered with dandelions and small weeds. "Close to the curb."

He started to speak but she cut him off when she opened her door and swung her feet out.

"I need to do this alone."

"Sure," he said quietly, "take your time."

He didn't understand why she left the vehicle door open before she walked toward the spot. Luke reached over to shut it, then decided to leave it alone. He wanted to hear her if she called to him.

She stood with her back to him, her arms wrapped around her waist, staring down at the ground. To Luke, it looked like any other weedy spot with no way to tell what had gone on there before today. After a few minutes, she came back to the vehicle, slid in, and shut the door. She sat silently, gazing dazedly at the floor.

Luke didn't know what to say. He wanted to comfort her but didn't have the slightest idea of how to approach her. "What are you feeling?" he said, at last, hoping he'd chosen the right words.

"Nothing." She shook her head slowly. "I feel nothing and I don't know why." She stared out the window while he started the car. "I need to go to the cemetery where Adam is buried."

He drove her to Lakewood Cemetery, a two-hundred-fifty-acre site in the heart of south Minneapolis. Luke had never been there and as he drove through the gates, past the administration building and the Byzantine-style chapel, he marveled at the sheer size and beauty of it. He'd always thought of cemeteries as peaceful and serene, but he found this place eerily quiet.

Jenny directed him to a section near a small lake on the east end of the cemetery. He pulled over to the side and shut off the Explorer, stretching out to make himself comfortable while he waited for her, but when she opened her door, she looked back and said, "Come with me."

Feeling strangely out of place, he did as she asked and left the vehicle, following her through a long stretch of imposing monuments and mature trees until they came to a row with a granite headstone made into a bench. As they walked toward it, Luke noticed an engraving along the edge of the seat. A small badge with the number 138 etched inside it accompanied the name "Officer Adam Russell Landon" on the left side. The words "End of Watch" and the date of his death appeared on the right. Luke stood back with his hands clasped together, paying his respects as Jenny knelt before her late husband's resting place with her head bowed.

Then she stood and slid her arms around Luke as though she needed something solid to hold her upright.

"My heart will always hold a special place for Adam," she said softly as she stared down at the gravestone. "Since he died, not a day has gone by that I haven't grieved over what happened to him." She sniffed and wiped her nose with a tissue from her jeans pocket. "But I can't do this any longer, Luke. I want to live for myself again." She looked up. "I want to love again."

He held her close, understanding exactly how she felt. He couldn't recall when it happened, whether it had been sudden or it had slowly grown over time, but he'd come to the same conclusion.

Turning back to the grave, she kissed her fingertips and leaned over, placing them lightly on the bench. Then she straightened. "I'm ready to go home, Luke."

Arm in arm, they walked back to his vehicle and drove away.

Luke's Explorer ambled toward the entrance, his mind lost in thought. He paid little attention to the large pickup truck driving into the cemetery at a fast clip. As it grew nearer, he slowed, concerned about the erratic swerving of the vehicle. He planned to turn right at the intersection to avoid passing it when it suddenly veered toward him. The landscape melted into a fast-moving blur as adrenaline shot through his limbs and his reflexes took over, working faster than his mind could compute.

The last thing Luke remembered was the pickup slamming into the Explorer. And Jenny's frantic scream.

***

The accident happened so fast that Jenny didn't have time to make sense of what was going on, much less brace herself for the crash.

Metal slammed against metal, windows exploded with a popping sound and the world turned upside-down as the SUV slammed against the curb and then flipped onto its roof on the grass.

"Jenny!" Luke bellowed once the vehicle stopped moving. "Are you okay?"

"I think so," she cried, hanging upside down inside her seatbelt. "But I need to get out of this thing!"

"Be careful!"

She couldn't see his face; his airbag had inflated. As it began to collapse, it hung between them. For some reason, hers hadn't activated, but she didn't stop to figure out why. All that mattered to her now was getting safely out of the car. She had to help Luke get out then find out what happened to the people in the other vehicle and call for medical assistance if they needed it.

Her side window had shattered from the force of the impact. She braced one hand against the roof to support her body and with the other, she struggled with the latch on her seatbelt. "I can't get it to release!"

The seatbelt unexpectedly gave way, causing her to fall on her hands, face, and chest. She began to crawl out her window by twisting and squeezing herself through the crumpled, compressed space. Pebble-sized pieces of glass fell from her hair and clothing onto the ground as she rolled over on the grass and rose to her hands and knees. Slowly, she climbed to her feet, using the side of the vehicle for support.

"Luke! I'm out!"

"Good! I'm working on it!"

The force of the impact had ejected her purse from the vehicle. She reached out and grabbed it to find her phone. Dumping it upside down, the contents spilled out—coins, gum, tissues, and makeup, but she still couldn't locate the one item she needed.

She managed to walk around the vehicle to the driver's side. "Luke!" She lowered to her hands and knees and tried to get the door open, but it wouldn't budge. "Are you okay?"

"Yeah," he said, trying to unlatch his seatbelt and break free. He suddenly broke loose, collapsing onto the roof with a thud. After a moment, he attempted to shimmy through the narrow space that used to be the window.

Jenny sat on the grass and gripped his hand, pulling him through the window until he could manage the rest of the way on his own.

"How are you doing?" she asked once he maneuvered himself to a sitting position. "Are you hurt?"

He sat on the ground with his back resting against the battered SUV. "I'm a little groggy from the airbag, but my head is clearing now." He pulled his phone from his back pocket. The case had cracked.

"Call 9-1-1," Jenny said. "I'm going to check on the other vehicle."

"Jenny, wait—"

Ignoring Luke's protest, she headed across the street toward the pickup truck. The front of the vehicle had been smashed in where it had broadsided the Explorer.

Fully alert now, she hustled to the pickup and opened the door. She found only one person—a man slumped over the steering wheel, his airbag deflated.

"Sir, can you hear me?"

The driver, a lean, weathered man with thinning hair, suddenly lifted his head. His bloodshot eyes struggled to focus. "Huh?" He reeked of alcohol.

Jenny took a step back and wrinkled her nose. "Sir, are you all right?"

He looked around, his face frowning in confusion. "Where am I? Wha-wha happened?"

"You've been in an accident. Are you in any pain?"

"An accident..." He glanced down at his seatbelt and tried to unbuckle it. "Get me out of this—" His head jerked around, his manner sobering at the sound of police sirens wailing in the distance.

"Sir, please, remain calm and stay in your vehicle. Help is on the way."

"You're crazy, lady." He glared at her and fumbled to free

himself. "I ain't got time to stick around."

"Sir, I said stay in the vehicle," Jenny ordered, automatically slipping into cop mode. "Help will be here at any moment now." She heard footsteps behind her and spun around.

"I called the police and they're on the way," Luke said walking toward the pickup.

The sirens were growing ear-splittingly loud. Red and blue lights flashed as a squad car sped through the entrance and raced toward the accident scene. Another unit followed close behind.

The man saw the flashing lights and jumped out of the pickup. In the process, he shoved Jenny aside, knocking her to the ground, and took off running.

Realizing what had happened, she scrambled to her feet and ran in pursuit of the drunk driver who was attempting to flee the scene.

"Jenny! Let him go!" Luke's frantic voice cut through the air, but his protest came too late. Glad she'd kept up her weekly strength training, she easily caught up to the man and tackled him to the ground, face down. Reaching to her belt for her handcuffs, she realized she didn't have any and it suddenly dawned on her that she was no longer a police officer.

"Hold still," she ordered as she grabbed his arm and held him. "I'm making a citizen's arrest!"

By then, Luke had reached her and helped her hold down the cursing, thrashing man until an officer ran toward them and took charge of the situation.

She stood up and started to walk away, but Luke spun her around, grabbing her by the shoulders. "Don't *ever* do that again! Do you understand me? You nearly gave me a heart attack!"

"Calm down, Luke," Jenny said defensively. "You know I've been professionally trained."

He took her by the arm and hustled her away from the action. "Look, I'm sorry. Maybe I did overreact, but when that pickup hit the Explorer and we went flying, I realized how easily I could lose you." He slid his arms protectively around her. "I've already lost the love of my life once. I'm not going through it a second time."

Her jaw dropped. "What did you say?"

He looked deep into her eyes. "I love you, Jenny."

Chapter Seven

One week before the wedding

The black SUV stretch limo Luke rented for Brandon's stag party pulled up to the front entrance of a popular Italian restaurant. The driver held the door while Luke and nearly a dozen casually dressed men climbed out. The men entered the restaurant and went straight to the bar, ordering drinks while they waited to be seated. Luke stood apart from the group and checked his phone. Only fifteen minutes had passed since the last time he'd looked at it.

This is going to be a long night...

Luke had talked one of the groomsmen, Marty Collins into helping him plan the bachelor party. He'd rented the stretch limo, fit for a king with a plush leather interior, wet bar, and extra legroom. Marty had arranged the schedule. He'd assured Luke that he'd taken care of all the details, but he didn't want to divulge much to keep the partygoers on the edge of their seats.

Not knowing the itinerary had kept Luke on the edge of his seat, all right, and on the edge of his sanity as well. The restaurant turned out to be a good choice, but what else did Marty have up his sleeve? Luke didn't like all the secrecy.

Brandon emerged from the crowd and handed him a drink. "Are

you seeing Jenny now?"

The day after the Kiss Cam incident, Luke had received the third degree from Brandon and a lecture about getting involved with his fiancée's sister. Since that conversation, Luke hadn't spoken to him about it. He didn't want Brandon's nose in his business—not the business of his love life, anyway.

"We usually walk the dogs together," Luke said, trying to sound casual. "Liam has ball games after school. She's helping me out with exercising the boxers we adopted from the shelter where she volunteers."

Brandon took a swig of his Jameson on the rocks. "You're seeing her every day? Aw, man, don't tell me you're—"

"You're right." Luke patted his best friend on the shoulder. "I'm not telling you. This is your party. We're supposed to be having fun."

Marty had reserved a private room so they could use salty language and speak freely without the worry of embarrassing themselves in front of the entire restaurant. Luke also didn't want bystanders uploading videos to social media of Brandon getting drunk.

"Why didn't you let me know you were serious about hooking up with a woman," Brandon said, ignoring Luke's attempt to change the subject as he followed Luke through the busy dining room. "I could have fixed you up with some of the most beautiful and sexy women you've ever met. All you had to do was ask."

Luke turned around. "What if I don't want to be *fixed up* with someone from your contact list? What if I want to do the *looking* myself?"

Brandon shrugged. "Well, in that case, you should've looked a little harder. I think you could have found someone classier than Jenny. And less wacky."

If Luke had to bet on which sister had a wackier personality, his wager wouldn't have been on Jenny. At least Jenny didn't make her day-to-day decisions based on what might affect her ratings at a job that was less secure than the janitorial staff at the station. He didn't harbor any dislike toward Heather. He simply couldn't see himself dating, much less marrying, someone as uptight and controlling as her.

He took a seat next to Brandon at the communal table set up for them to eat spaghetti and meatballs "family" style. "This is your big night, Brandon," Luke said loudly and banged a spoon against his glass to garner the group's attention. "It's Brandon's last hurrah. Let's start it out with a toast." He held up his glass. "To the groom, who has an appointment tomorrow, regardless of his hangover, to get fitted for his custom-made ball and chain." A chorus of laughter and cheers erupted around the table.

After dinner, the group filed back into the limo and went to a casino for some Cosmic Blackjack and a "killer" comedy show. They hit the bar for a "farewell to my money" drink and then headed back to the limo for Marty's special evening finale.

Twenty minutes later, the limo pulled up to a brick building with no visible sign and a poorly lit parking lot filled with cars. Luke had questioned Marty earlier in the evening about their final event and Marty's evasiveness had given him a bad feeling. As soon as he entered the dark, windowless room filled with men and saw the strobe lights flashing, he knew why Marty had kept it a secret. Had Luke known, he would never have agreed. The last thing Brandon needed was an amateur video on Facebook or YouTube showing him drunk and disorderly while getting a lap dance. The marriage would be over before it started. So would his career.

He pulled out his phone with the cracked case to call the limo driver, but Brandon snatched it away. "No distractions allowed tonight. We're here to party!" Brandon already had so much to drink he was beginning to stagger.

Luke grabbed his phone back, wishing he could wring Marty's

neck. He didn't want to be in this joint and he didn't want Jenny to find out that he'd been here, either. As a former cop, she'd probably had her share of calls to places like this and saw things he could only imagine. He didn't want her to think he preferred this type of entertainment when he went out with his friends.

He suddenly missed her and wished he could leave right now. He wanted to be with her, to take her out for a quiet evening instead of playing chaperone to a bunch of drunks acting like idiots. He never imagined he'd fall in love again, especially with someone the total opposite of Mara. True love didn't get an encore, or so he'd once thought. But he'd been wrong. It did happen again and it got even better the second time around.

A fight broke out on the other side of the room over one of the girls. Luke squared his shoulders and plowed through the crowd, hoping none of his people were involved.

Yep, it's gonna be a long night...

***

"Liam! The pizza is here!"

Jenny tipped the delivery boy and shut the living room door. The pungent aroma of a sixteen-inch sausage pizza with extra cheese permeated Luke's three-bedroom house and made her mouth water. She hadn't had a pizza that smelled this fantastic in a long time.

"Liam!" She shouted down the basement stairs. "Come up here before it gets cold."

She busied herself setting the table with small plates and napkins while she waited for him to emerge from his teenage man cave in the basement. Eventually, she heard his gunboat-sized tennis shoes shuffling on the stairs followed by the padded thumping of dog paws behind him. He appeared in the kitchen wearing jeans, a black T-shirt, and the same green Army-style jacket he'd had on at the shelter. She didn't know why he needed to wear a coat to the dinner table on a beautiful spring evening, but she ignored it, choosing to focus on the food instead.

She opened the refrigerator. "Would you like a Coke?"

He grunted an answer and helped himself to a wedge-shaped slice of pizza, eating it with his fingers.

She took out two chilled cans and set them on the round, wooden table. "Does it taste as good as it smells?"

He nodded without looking at her and continued stuffing his mouth.

What happened to the handsome kid with the deep voice and snarky sense of humor she'd encountered the last time she'd visited this house?

She helped herself to a piece of pizza and set it on her plate. She always ate it with a knife and fork but changed her mind and picked it up with her hands, taking a large bite.

When in Rome...

They ate their pizza and drank the Cokes. The snap and fizz of pulling off the tabs made the only sound in the kitchen. That and the tapping of claws on the tile floor as the dogs sat by Liam's chair, waiting impatiently for their share of his leftovers.

"So, are you and my dad...you know...making permanent plans?" he demanded suddenly. His angry tone made the question sound more like an accusation.

"We enjoy each other's company," Jenny said quietly. "We haven't discussed anything beyond that."

"He used to love my mom," Liam said and stared at her as though she'd committed a moral crime by befriending Luke. "I guess now that he's got you, he's forgotten about her."

"That's not true, Liam." She picked up her pizza and noticed her

85

hand was shaking. She set it back down. "He hasn't forgotten her at all. She'll always be in his heart."

His amber eyes pierced hers with hurt and confusion. "Then what does that make you?"

"His friend."

"You didn't look like friends to me on the Kiss Cam."

His accusation left her speechless.

He stood up and tossed a couple of discarded crusts to the dogs then walked to the door.

Her heart began to slam at the thought of Liam taking off. "Where are you going?"

"The garage—to play my guitar."

He slammed the door and left her to clean up the kitchen alone. Almost immediately, she heard him practicing out in the garage, although, *plunking* more accurately described it.

She began cleaning up the mess, tossing paper napkins into the empty pizza box. Crumbs covered the table along with a few greasy smudges. She looked for a dishcloth around the sink but didn't find any. As she pulled open drawers, searching for the kitchen linens, she found tablecloths and placemats, baking utensils, and a drawer filled with table runners for every season and holiday. These items belonged to Mara and the way they had been neatly folded suggested no one had disturbed them since she passed.

Jenny slowly closed the drawer. Somehow, it didn't feel right to disturb her things.

Instead, she grabbed a sheet of paper towel and wet it down. As she wiped the table with it, she looked up and saw a framed photograph on the wall of Luke, Mara, and Liam sitting on a rough-hewn bench wearing T-shirts and shorts. Behind them, the wide caldera filled with the deep blue water of Crater Lake contrasted against jagged cliffs covered with tall evergreens. Liam, who looked to be about seven, sat between his parents, squinting because of the bright sun on his face.

It must have been so difficult for him to lose his mom... Her heart went out to him.

She began cleaning the table again, determined to reach out to Liam and hopefully, become friends.

After straightening up, she walked outside and stood for a moment at the service door, wondering what to say. When she opened the door, he stopped playing and stared at her, letting her know he didn't appreciate her trespassing on his private domain.

"Have you had lessons?"

He shook his head, giving her an irascible glare that silently said, *What's it to you?*

"I can tell." She looked over the guitar. "If you want to be good on that thing you need to get the basics down and practice every day."

He tipped his head, frowning. "What would you know about it?"

"I played on a Fender in high school."

His jaw dropped. "In a rock band?"

"Well, yeah." She raised her hands. "Didn't everybody?"

Liam's scowl turned into wide-eyed interest. "What kind of music did you play?"

"Prince, who else?" She said dreamily, laying one hand over her heart. "I loved His Purple Majesty."

Liam pulled the strap over his head and handed the guitar to Jenny. "Play something."

Okay, baby, let me show you how this is done...

Jenny slid the strap over her shoulder and mentally prepared herself to sing "Let's Go Crazy," her favorite Prince tune of all time.

She sang into the microphone in a throaty voice and raised her arm the way she'd seen Prince do it many times. She jumped into the song, dancing side to side and spinning around, enjoying the thrill of performing as she did at sixteen. Before long, Liam climbed on his drums and began playing along with her, tossing his dark, wavy hair as he pounded his sticks.

When she finished the song, she bent over, gasping for breath. "I'm going to die..."

"Come on, do another one," Liam coaxed and began to show off on his drums.

Realizing they'd found common ground, Jenny sucked in her breath and began to sing again, belting out "I Would Die 4 You," "Purple Rain" and "Baby I'm a Star." As she sang, she thought of Prince dancing around in his tight, button-down pants and ruffled white shirt, his curly black hair bouncing with each step. She couldn't get close to his unique style but it sure was a blast trying.

They were having so much fun they didn't realize how much noise they were generating until Grandpa Munster burst through the service door. The sight of him in his balloon-like pants with suspenders caused Jenny to hit a stray cord before she ceased playing altogether.

"Don't stop now," he said and pressed the button to open the overhead garage door. "Youse was doing good." The door rolled up, revealing the neighbors sitting on their porches, including an elderly woman with curly, lavender hair. "See, we don't care if you play," Grandpa Munster said, smiling, "as long as it's sumthin' good."

They played until ten o'clock, covering every song Jenny knew and they even convinced Grandpa Munster to take the microphone and sing "The House on The Rising Sun." Once the neighbors heard that, they began to retreat inside their homes.

"Hey," Liam said at ten o'clock as he closed the overhead door, "do you want to watch a movie?"

"Sure." Jenny set the guitar back in its case. "What do you have on DVD?"

"DVD?" Liam laughed. "Who watches movies like that? I've got Netflix."

They turned off the interior light and went into the house. Once they decided which movie to stream, they made a couple of bags of microwave popcorn to munch on and claimed their spots on the sofa.

Jenny didn't realize she'd fallen asleep until someone woke her with a gentle kiss on the lips.

"Hey there, Sleeping Beauty," Luke whispered. His mussed hair and disheveled clothing made him look like he'd been in a bar brawl. "How'd it go?"

"What?" Her dry, sore throat made the word sound like a croak. As she sat up, a multi-colored afghan slid off her and dropped to the living room floor. "We had a good time." She looked around. "Where's Liam? He was right here—"

Oh-oh, did he take off after I fell asleep?

Luke left her and went downstairs but returned quickly. "He's sleeping in his bed with the hounds. I told him to get up. They need to go outside for their morning run." He planted a kiss on her forehead, the rough stubble on his chin brushing against her soft skin. "Then we're *all* going out for breakfast."

"Sure," Jenny said and collapsed on the sofa, closing her eyes again. She didn't need breakfast. She needed a transfusion of Red Bull. And she needed to get that music out of her head.

Let's go crazy...

Chapter Eight

The wedding day

"You're going to survive this day, Brandon." Luke bolstered his wedding day pep talk to the lucky groom with a light pat on the back. They stood in the groom's lounge at the historic LaSalle Mansion getting ready for the wedding ceremony. "Every groom does."

Brandon's face reflected a green tinge, indicating he might puke at any moment. His fingers shook as he tried to slip the cufflink through the stiff fabric of his starched white shirt. He'd chosen to go with a black designer suit in his favorite label instead of a tuxedo. A matching suit cost Luke several times over what he preferred to spend, but he considered the money worth it to avoid wearing a tuxedo, the main object that reminded Jenny of the day her husband died.

"Let me do that." Luke took the gold cufflinks out of his fumbling hands. "Hold still."

Marty Collins walked into the groom's lounge concealing a lowball glass with a double shot of Jameson on the rocks underneath a cloth napkin. "Here." He shoved the glass into Brandon's free hand. "This oughta loosen you up and settle your nerves."

"Fine," Luke said as he finished the last cuff, "but that's his limit. We don't want him getting too loose before he walks down the aisle."

Marty plopped on the sofa, stretching his chunky arm across the back. His unruly reddish curls flopped across his forehead. "Look, Brandon, you're going to be fine."

Brandon leaned against the pool table, gripping the edge with white-knuckled hands. "What if I'm making a mistake?"

"What makes you think that?" Luke asked as he stood in front of the mirror checking his own tie and straightening his cuffs.

"I don't know," Brandon replied in a worried tone. His usual abundance of self-confidence appeared to be taking quite a hit. "I guess I've got the wedding day jitters."

Someone knocked on the door. Everyone froze. One of the ushers poked his head in. "The wedding coordinator sent me to tell you it's time to go."

Brandon gulped the rest of his drink while Luke straightened Brandon's boutonniere, a blush rose with baby's breath accented with a miniature golf club charm.

The men made their way to the entrance of the secluded outdoor courtyard where two hundred guests sat amid the lush foliage and café lights, waiting for the ceremony to begin. In the front row, Heather's personal assistant sat holding Princess, a wedding gift to Heather from Jenny.

"Don't be nervous," Luke said to Brandon. "Once you see your beautiful bride, you'll forget about everything else."

The music started. They listened for their cue and then took "the walk" toward the lighted arch under a canopy of tall, shady trees.

Luke stood next to Brandon at the altar, waiting for the bridal procession to start. The bridesmaids made their entrance and took their place at the altar.

The moment he saw Jenny, he couldn't take his gaze off her. She wore a long, strapless dress in magenta and carried a matching nosegay of roses. She'd had her hair styled in an elaborate braid with baby's breath woven along the sides.

"When it's your turn, don't look around," he'd told her at the rehearsal, "just focus on me."

She slowly walked down the aisle, her face alight with a beautiful smile. No one but him knew how much she struggled to keep from panicking. His gaze locked on hers, giving her encouragement until she'd completed the journey and taken her place at the front.

The ring bearer came next, followed by the flower girls, sprinkling magenta rose petals as they went.

The cue came announcing the bride and everyone stood. Heather made her way to the altar with the air of a queen in a flowing, white lace dress that bared her shoulders. She held a bouquet of magenta roses. Her hair, swept into a knot at her nape and accented with miniature roses, completed the stunning look.

Luke stole a sideways glance at the groom and breathed a sigh of relief. Brandon stood transfixed, smiling at his bride with stars in his eyes.

So far, this wedding had gone off without a hitch, but Luke couldn't let his guard down yet. They still had to get through the reception.

***

After the ceremony, Jenny collapsed into Luke's arms. "I did it! I'm so relieved! Now, I just have to get through the reception."

He gave her a bear hug. "I knew you could do it. You're stronger than you think."

She hugged him back, not caring if she smudged her makeup or mussed her hair. She loved the strength of his arms around her, the way he made her feel, and that was all that mattered.

Heather and I—what a pair, she thought, laying her cheek on Luke's shoulder. *I didn't panic and she didn't faint. Someday we'll look back on this day and laugh, but right now I'm just grateful I'm getting through it without a disaster.*

The wedding party spent the next hour posing for the photographer while the guests enjoyed an outdoor cocktail reception. After that, the staff ushered everyone into the ballroom for dinner. Jenny sat at the head table next to Luke and dined on chicken roulade with oven-roasted asparagus and garlic potatoes. During the meal, Luke angled his head and whispered in her ear, "You look beautiful." They smiled at each other and held hands under the table. She couldn't remember the last time she'd been this happy.

The grand finale took place in the Carriage House. The two-story building had a wooden dance floor and a second-floor mezzanine where people could sit on the sofas to visit or simply stand at the rail and watch the dance party going on below.

Jenny held hands with Luke all evening, mixing with guests and dancing to a live quartet.

"Hey," Luke said to her as they sat out one dance and sipped on glasses of ice water. "How are you holding up?"

"I'm doing great." She laid her head on his shoulder. "I'm right where I want to be—with you."

Luke smiled and hugged her.

Toward the end of the evening, Jenny wandered away from Luke for a few minutes to visit with relatives, but when she looked for him again, he was nowhere around. Gathering her wristlet handbag, she sought out her sister and found Heather on the mezzanine level chatting with a group of friends. Princess sat obediently on Heather's lap.

Easing her way through the crowd, Jenny waved to get Heather's attention. "Have you seen Luke?"

Heather laughed at something one of the women sitting with her said before turning her attention to Jenny. "No, but if you find him, you'll probably come across *my husband*, too. I haven't seen either of them for a while."

Jenny left Heather and struck out on her own to find Luke. After a few minutes of wandering through one corridor after another, she discovered a stairway encased in richly paneled walls and took the stairs to the next level. She followed the open corridor into another section and suddenly heard heated voices coming from behind a partially closed door. The plate on the door indicated she'd found the groom's lounge. The voices, she swiftly realized, belonged to Luke and Brandon.

"She's not right for you, Luke," Brandon said earnestly, almost pleading with him. "You're making a huge mistake."

"You're drunk," she heard Luke retort. "You don't know what you're talking about."

Shocked by the emotion in their voices, Jenny silently pushed the door open wide enough to see into the room. Luke stood with his back to Brandon, leaning over the fireplace. Brandon paced the room holding a drink.

"I know exactly what I'm talking about because I've known her longer than you have," Brandon said. "I was there when she went off the rails."

They're talking about me, Jenny thought as her heart vaulted to her throat.

Luke spun around to argue, but Brandon cut him off. "You've had a few weeks of fun with her, but it's time to let her go. I'm telling you, Luke, you can't get mixed up with Jenny Landon. She'll only cause you pain."

"You're wrong, Brandon." Luke's face flushed with anger. "Jenny has had her share of tough times, but she's put them behind her now. You don't know her like I do. She's a caring, loving woman."

Brandon countered with a frustrated laugh. "Caring and loving don't add up to emotionally stable. She seems normal right now because everything is going her way, but drop a small crisis into the mix, like simply asking her to be in the wedding and she falls apart. Don't deny it." Brandon slammed his drink on the pool table. "You were sitting right next to her the night of the engagement party. You saw how she acted."

"You're right—I did, but our being together has changed her. It's changed *me*." Luke jerked at his necktie and loosened it, as though he couldn't breathe. "What's the matter with you, Brandon? Why are you attacking your sister-in-law like this? She doesn't deserve it and frankly, neither do I. I thought we were friends."

"Luke," Brandon argued, "listen to me! It's because we're friends and because I care about your happiness that I can't let this go." Brandon leaned both hands on the felt surface, facing Luke across the pool table. "Look, I saw what you went through with Mara, week after week, month after month. It nearly tore you apart. I can't stand by and watch you go through another heartache."

Brandon's words cut through Jenny's heart, making her feel like the crazy person he'd described. She'd never considered how deeply Mara's illness had wounded Luke and how much he had suffered. Brandon was right. Luke was a good man and he needed a strong woman to support him, not someone weak and tortured like her. Not someone who couldn't even get through her sister's wedding without his help. Shame and humiliation washed over her like a tsunami.

Heartsick over the truth, she leaned against the door as her eyes filled with tears. It moved, causing the hinges to squeak.

Both men spun around and saw her standing in the doorway.

"He's right, Luke," she said with tears spilling down her face. "It will never work between us. You need someone to build you up. I'll only bring you down."

"Jenny, no! That's not true—"

She couldn't face him and listen to his excuses. Kicking off her shoes, she picked up her skirt and fled down the hallway running as fast as she could. A small group of people had congregated on the stairs. Sobbing, she brushed past them, taking the stairs two at a time, and kept running until she found her way to the front door. Across the street, a Yellow Cab sat with its motor running. She raced toward it and jumped in.

"Take me home! I have to leave now!"

Jenny shut her phone off to keep Luke from calling or texting. Her fragile world had collapsed and she couldn't face him ever again. Feeling utterly alone, she cried her heart out all the way home.

Chapter Nine

Two weeks after the wedding

Luke pushed open the back door and stepped out onto the deck. "Liam, bring the dogs into the house and get changed. I want to get to the concert in plenty of time to find a decent parking space. The traffic is going to be bumper-to-bumper." They were going to an outdoor concert at the Como Lakeside Pavilion at Como Park in St. Paul.

Liam stood in the backyard in ripped jeans and a faded green tank top, throwing sticks for the dogs to fetch. He whistled to his four-legged companions and headed for the house.

Luke went back into the kitchen and began filling a small red and white cooler with cans of soda. He heard the thundering of paws on the deck just before the dogs burst into the house through their private pet door and bounded down the basement stairs. Moments later, the back door opened and Liam appeared.

"We'll get something to eat at the park," Luke said to him as he pulled a large bag of ice from the freezer. "I hear they've got a lot of new vendors this year. I'm hungry for tacos. What about you?"

Liam paused at the basement doorway and shrugged. "Why don't you call Jenny and ask her to meet us there?"

Luke stiffened, his spine more rigid than the ice in his hands. Ever since Liam found out that he and Jenny had parted ways, the boy had stubbornly refused to accept it. He'd grown to like Jenny more than Luke had realized. "You know we're not seeing each other any longer."

Liam responded with an impatient sigh. "What's the matter with you, Dad? Why don't you just talk to her and straighten things out?"

"I've tried repeatedly," Luke argued as he tore a hole in the bag and dumped half of the ice into the cooler. "She won't answer my calls or my texts. I've gone to her house, but she doesn't answer the door."

"Why?" His son gripped the door frame, giving him an accusing glare. "What did you do to make her hate you so much—cheat on her?"

"Give me a break. You know I'd never do that," Luke snapped as he jerked open the freezer and shoved the bag inside. Even so, he understood Liam's frustration. He'd been dealing with it himself ever since the wedding. He missed Jenny so much he couldn't stop thinking about her or struggling with regret over the way it happened. Jenny's reasons for their breakup, however, were private, and in his mind, repeating them to anyone else without her permission would amount to betraying her confidence. He slammed the freezer door shut. "It just…didn't work out."

"I don't believe you," Liam said, raising his voice. "She *liked* you, Dad, and you liked her. The whole neighborhood told me about you two makin' out in the driveway."

The memory of that day replayed in his mind, filling his soul with profound sadness. He could still smell the sweet fragrance of her skin as he held her in his arms and the silky texture of her long, blonde hair fluttering in the breeze, brushing against his face. Her eyes were so blue, her lips so soft…

"Look, I…" He leaned against the kitchen counter and stared at the floor, massaging the back of his neck. It ached from tension and the countless sleepless nights he'd been through, trying to sort out what he could have done differently; what he *should* have done differently. "I know it's difficult to understand, but it was Jenny's decision, not mine. It's over between us and there's nothing I can do to change that." He looked up. "I'm sorry, that's just the way it is."

For a moment, neither spoke.

"All I know is," Liam said solemnly, giving him a long, serious look, "if I was in love with a girl like her, I'd *never* give up." Instead of waiting for a reaction from his father, he charged down the basement stairs, leaving Luke alone in the kitchen to mull over his words.

Placing the palm of his hand on the table for support, Luke closed his eyes and slowly drew in a deep breath. Liam had unknowingly described what he'd been struggling with ever since that fateful night Jenny left the wedding without him. He loved her so much his heart wouldn't give her up and not being able to even talk to her was tearing him apart. He had to see her again; he had to find some way to convince her to put that night behind them and start over.

What if she refused?

That was a chance he was willing to take.

***

Jenny peered through a bedroom window on the second floor of her home, staring down at Brandon as he leaned on her doorbell. He stood alone, prompting her to wonder why Heather wasn't with him. He'd never been to her house before without her sister.

She unlocked the window and lifted the lower panel. The searing June heat wafted through the screen. "Brandon, is something wrong? Where's Heather?"

At the sound of her voice, he looked up. "She's at the mall, shopping for baby furniture." He placed his hands on his hips. "Jenny, I need to talk to you."

The serious tone in his voice put her on edge. After all the grief he'd caused her at the wedding, he had a lot of nerve showing up at her door demanding to see her. "What is this about?"

He glanced around, checking to see if anyone overheard him. "May I come in? It's private."

Oh-oh, here it comes, she thought wryly. *He's here to accuse me of leaking Heather's secret to the public, but I didn't do it!*

She sighed and closed the window. Once downstairs, she swung open the front door. Brandon stood at the threshold wearing navy Brooks Brothers chinos and a blue plaid short-sleeved shirt.

"This is about the baby, isn't it?" She demanded as she stood aside to let him in. "Heather asked me not to tell anyone and I've kept my promise. I swear I don't know how the information leaked out."

Ignoring her question, he walked into her living room and glanced around, looking uncomfortable. Brandon never got nervous, at least not around her, and his uncharacteristic behavior made her tense. If he hadn't made the trip to interrogate her about how news of Heather's pregnancy had landed on the front page of the Sunday paper's variety section, then what did he want? Something was up…

She stood with her hand on the door, keeping it open to usher him back through it once he'd finished announcing whatever bombshell he'd come to drop. "If this isn't about Heather, then what's the matter?" The moment she spoke, she realized it had to be about Luke. She shut the door and folded her arms across her chest. "Brandon—"

"I want to apologize for my behavior at the wedding," he said quickly, cutting her off. "The things I said about you were uncalled for."

Her mouth gaped. Heather must have put him up to this to make amends. Even though he'd recited all the appropriate words, he didn't bother trying to sound sorry and it made her mad. "What's there to apologize for now? Thanks to you, the damage has already been done."

"Jenny, I know you think I came between you and Luke at the wedding because I have a grudge against you, but you're wrong."

Her spine stiffened as a wave of indignation surged through her. "Oh, really? It sure sounded to me like you harbored a grudge."

He blinked, taken aback by her reaction. "Okay, I admit I was a bit harsh. I intervened because Luke has been through a lot and I don't want to see him hurt again." Though he tried to sound sympathetic this time, his face still showed no emotion. "He's like a brother to me."

"Oh," she fired back, "so, you took it upon yourself to save poor, helpless Luke from that evil witch, Jenny?"

"Of course not. I didn't mean it that way. Look, I realize that losing your husband has been tough on you and you've had a difficult time coping with the situation." Brandon placed his broad hands on her shoulders. "But you have *no idea* what Luke went through."

"Is that so?" She stepped back, pulling away from him. She didn't want his empathy. "How would you know whether I do or not?"

His eyes narrowed at her persistent sarcasm. This little scene was obviously not going the way he'd planned. "Because if you'd known the truth about Mara, you would have understood where my concern for Luke was coming from."

Something in the way he said *Mara* sparked her curiosity. "What do you mean?"

"Luke and Mara were the perfect couple," Brandon stated with brutal honesty. "Totally inseparable. Luke was so much in love with her that it changed him completely. He stopped drinking with the guys, started a business, and built a house for her after she had Liam." Brandon's sand-colored brows furrowed. "Then Mara got cancer."

Shocked, Jenny dropped her arms to her sides and stared at him. "Are you saying she had cancer more than once?"

He nodded. "She had a hysterectomy the first time."

Jenny didn't know if she had the air-conditioning turned down too far or if Brandon's words had affected her more than she realized, but she began to shiver. Reaching into the coat closet, she pulled out a long sweater and quickly slid her arms into it. "Luke never talked about his wife and I didn't think it appropriate to ask about her."

Brandon seemed oblivious to the chill in the room. "Mara kept getting sick," he continued. "Eventually, she was diagnosed with pancreatic cancer. The chemotherapy seemed to be working for a while, but in time, her cancer came back and it was worse than before."

"Gosh, that must have been heartbreaking," Jenny said, wondering how Luke kept all this inside him without going crazy.

"He kept a cheerful attitude," Brandon said, "even though he was breaking apart inside. He knew he was losing her and he couldn't do a thing about it, but he never let it show because he didn't want her last days to be marred by his sadness."

"What's the point of telling me all of this?" Pulling the thick sweater tighter around her, she wrapped the matching belt around her waist and tied it. "What difference does it make now?"

"My point is," he said bluntly, "Luke's one of the toughest guys I know, but he needs a woman who'll lift him up, not pull him down."

The insinuation was clear. He was apologizing to make peace in the family, but he hadn't changed his opinion of her or his belief that Luke was better off without her.

It wasn't enough to stick a knife in my heart, you're bent on twisting it, too.

She opened the door and stood aside for him to leave. "Thank you for confiding in me about Luke," she said evenly, feigning politeness. "I appreciate your honesty." She really wanted to verbally rip his head off and order him out of her house but held her tongue for Heather's sake. She didn't want to be the cause of any division between Heather and her new husband.

As for Luke, Brandon was right. Luke needed a woman without serious baggage. He deserved someone who would "lift him up" and bring joy into his life, not someone as broken as her. She'd always be grateful for how he'd helped her come to terms with Adam's murder and find peace so she could get on with her life. She wished him well.

She waited until Brandon left and she'd closed the door on their chilly confrontation before letting go. Leaning against the door, her eyes filled with tears at the thought of never being with Luke again—never slipping her hand into his, never feeling the gentle strength of his arms around her, never again enjoying the passion of his kiss.

She thought about the day he'd kissed her as they lounged against her car in his driveway. She'd fallen in love with him in the flutter of a heartbeat, never realizing the issues that haunted her past would one day become the barrier that blocked their future together. Words couldn't express the agony she felt now, but the tears flowing down her face silently confirmed it. She would always love Luke and hoped with all her heart that one day he would be truly happy again.

She gave herself a few minutes to indulge in her little pity party then wiped her cheeks with the back of her hands and walked into the bathroom to wash her face.

Jackie Boy sprang to the vanity top and huddled his furry, black and white body in front of his water dish sitting to one side of the faucet. Jenny turned on the water and watched him study it with curiosity.

"I think it's time to get on with my life," she said to him as she petted his soft coat. "I've been putting it off long enough. I need something to do. Something different and challenging." She scratched under his white chin, embellished with a smudge of black. "What do you have to say about that, puddy tat?"

Jackie Boy lifted his head and purred his approval.

Chapter Ten

Four weeks after the wedding

Jenny lay on the beige leather sofa in her living room with Jackie Boy curled up next to her, mulling over her future.

"I think it's time we sell this house," she said to Jackie Boy. "Now that all of our foster dogs have found forever homes and I'm not taking any more, the place is too big for us, wouldn't you say?"

Jackie Boy loudly purred his consent.

It had been a month since the wedding. Luke had called repeatedly and left at least a dozen messages on her phone until she'd blocked his number. Talking to him might give him the idea that reconciliation was possible and she didn't want to hurt him or herself any worse than she already had.

The break with Luke had proven to be one of the most difficult decisions she'd ever made, but being with him—loving him—had changed her forever. She realized that Minneapolis held too many memories and she wanted a fresh start. She'd resigned from her position at the shelter and found adoptive families for all of the foster dogs in her care. Listing her four-bedroom house with a realtor sounded like a sensible idea. Moving somewhere warm and far away where she could start over sounded even better.

Her cell phone rang. She picked it up and checked the number. "Hi, Heather. How are you?"

"Princess wants to say hello to you," Heather said, sounding like a mother talking about her adorable child. "Say hi to Auntie Jenny, Princess. Come on, baby."

Jenny sighed and stared at the ceiling, wondering how to break the news to her sister.

"What's the matter? You sound preoccupied," Heather said, breaking into her thoughts. "You're still upset with Brandon, aren't you? Jenny, you know how sorry I am about what happened. I'm going to make it up to you. I promise."

"No, I'm not upset—at least, not anymore. Brandon has a right to his opinion and I accept that." Though she tried to sound calm and in control, her stomach clenched. She closed her eyes, willing herself to keep her voice even. "Going our separate ways isn't how I had envisioned things would turn out between Luke and me, but that's where we're at, so let's move on. Besides, I have some exciting news."

"Really?" Heather's rushed reply sounded forced, as though she was relieved to change the subject. "What is it? Do you have a date tonight?"

"Yeah, with Jackie Boy! We're going to watch a movie." Jenny laughed. "Actually, I'm contemplating selling my house and moving to California. There is a terrific school out there for training search dog teams."

"What?" Heather gasped. "No, you can't do that!"

"Why not? It's time for a change of scenery. Joining a volunteer search and rescue unit is something I've always wanted to do. Besides, California is only a couple of hours away by plane."

Heather smacked her lips. "If you want new scenery, I'll buy you some plants."

Jenny laughed so hard that she scared Jackie Boy. He jumped off the sofa and ran into the kitchen to wait for her by his food dish. "Did you call to talk about something in particular, sis?"

"Well, since I can't go jogging anymore until after the baby comes, I thought we could do something else together."

"Okay. What did you have in mind?"

Heather hesitated. "How about going to a Twins game?"

Jenny sat up. The thought of going back to Target Field, to the place where she and Luke first kissed touched a tender spot in her heart. "That's not a good idea. Those seats are pretty hard and you're always complaining about the ache in your back."

"I'll bring a pillow," Heather said dryly. "How does tomorrow afternoon sound? The game starts at noon. I'll get tickets for some good seats close to the field and have yours waiting at the Will Call booth."

Jenny lay back down and stared at the ceiling again. "Are you sure about this?"

"Yes! I'm craving a hot dog."

"You're not supposed to eat junk like that now."

Heather laughed. "That's why it tastes so-o-o-o good. I'll see you tomorrow. I've got a little surprise for you. Don't be late!"

***

Luke stood at the top row of the section, struggling to work up the nerve to approach her. Given her propensity to be late, he'd waited until the game started so there was no chance they'd accidentally bump into each other in this area of the stadium. He didn't know what would happen when she saw him, but he knew he had to give Heather's idea a chance. Every other method he'd tried to reach out to Jenny had failed.

He started down the stairs, keeping an eye on her as he approached. Target Field had many empty seats today so she wasn't difficult to locate. She wore the gray and navy Twins shirt, the one she'd purchased at the clubhouse store. The red ribbon tied into a bow around her ponytail made her look like the cutest tomboy he'd ever seen. She held the phone to her ear, probably chewing out her sister for not showing up.

He stopped one row behind her and stared at her back. His stomach flip-flopped at the prospect of looking into her eyes, of hearing her voice.

Speak now, buddy, or spend the rest of your life in regret for not at least trying...

His heart jumped to his throat as he stepped into her view. She stopped talking on the phone and simply stared.

"Jenny, please don't tell me to leave. Just give me a chance to say what's on my heart. Once you hear me out, if you still don't want anything to do with me, I promise, I'll never bother you again."

Her hand holding the phone dropped to her lap as she disconnected the call, but she didn't move to get up. "There's nothing to talk about, Luke."

Not a good conversation starter.

His palms began to sweat. "How about I go first?" He took a deep breath and spilled his guts. "I still love you. More than ever."

Her face paled.

The Twins scored a home run and the roar of the crowd rose to a deafening level.

"I'll say it again," he said, ignoring the craziness going on around them. "I love you, Jenny, and I miss you. I can't live without you." He sat in the empty seat next to her then reached over and took her hand. It was shaking as badly as his was and the realization that he might be getting through to her gave him the courage to continue. "I need the answer to something that has been bothering me since it happened. Why did you run away from me that night? Why didn't you give me the chance to make things right?"

Her eyes filled with tears. "Everything Brandon said about me was true. I'm broken."

"Look, if going through a difficult time dealing with the death of your spouse means you're broken, then I'm broken, too." Luke lifted his hand to her face, wiping away the moisture from her cheeks with the backs of his fingers. "It's not easy to let go of someone you love. It's downright impossible to understand why the Lord took my wife and your husband away from us." His fingers gently tilted her face upward until their lips were but a breath apart. "I had to let Mara go because there was nothing I could do to keep her from slipping away, but as long as I have a breath in me, I figure I have a fighting chance to get you back. So, I'm not going to give up. I *can't* give up."

He swallowed hard, desperate to make her understand that his feelings for her were unconditional. "I need you, Jenny. You're the light of my life. From the first moment I saw you, black eye and all, something in my heart stirred and I couldn't get you out of my mind. You and I were meant to be together."

She began to cry again. "I've never stopped loving you, but after hearing what Brandon said, I figured you were better off without me and I simply pushed you away. That way it didn't hurt so much."

He pulled her close, whispering in her ear, "Don't cry, honey. I'll never let anyone hurt you ever again."

He kissed her slowly at first, taking his time, savoring the taste of her lips. He wanted to make sure she welcomed his touch. His heart leaped for joy when she slid her arms around his neck and leaned into his kiss. They sat together with their arms around each other, quietly enjoying each other's company.

When the sixth inning rolled around, Luke kept a close watch on the scoreboard, hoping everything went along as he'd planned. The Kiss Cam flashed on the screen and began catching one couple after another by surprise. When it landed on them, he began to shake so badly he didn't know if he could go through with it. Could he pull this off without making a fool of himself? Would she say yes and make him the happiest man in the world? Forcing himself to swallow his fear, he got down on one knee and shakily pulled a white velvet box from his pocket. He opened it to reveal a sparkling diamond ring and held the box out to her. Then taking her hand in his he said, "Will you marry me, Jenny?"

She didn't answer at first. Her gaze widened, riveted on the ring.

Sweat began to form on his upper lip. "J-Jenny?"

Suddenly, she looked up. And smiled through fresh tears pooling in her eyes, but this time they were generated by her happiness. "Yes," she said, barely able to speak. "Yes! I do. I mean, I-I will!"

All around them, people cheered over their special moment. The group of elderly ladies occupying the seats in front of them turned around and profusely congratulated them. One lady asked, "Are you going to have a big wedding?"

Luke and Jenny studied each other's faces for a moment then shouted at the same time, "No way!"

Chapter Eleven

Four months later…

Jenny and Luke's wedding day

The setting Hawaiian sun hung suspended over the horizon like a giant ball of fire as Jenny joined together with Luke in a small wedding chapel on the island of Kauai. Their quaint hotel, located on the outskirts of Princeville, provided an idyllic place for exchanging their wedding vows. Luke showed off his new blue and white Aloha shirt. Jenny wore a white sleeveless dress with a lace bodice.

No fuss, no fanfare, just the two of us in our own little world for the next ten days, Jenny thought dreamily as she took her place beside Luke.

Reverend Lani, an older gentleman with white hair and a trim beard, sang a song in Hawaiian and blew on his conch shell before guiding them through the ceremony. His wife stood off to one side in a multi-colored muumuu, holding up Luke's new iPhone so that Liam, the dogs, and both their families could watch the ceremony from his house via "Facetime."

Reverend Lani recited the "Verse by the Sea" as they held hands. When he finished, Jenny and Luke offered each other a colorful lei of alternating white plumeria and purple orchid, the Hawaiian symbol of love. He guided them through their Declaration of Intention, Marriage Vows, and the exchange of their rings.

"I now pronounce you man and wife," Reverend Lani said after he recited the Prayer of Blessings in Hawaiian. He nodded to Luke. "You may kiss your bride."

"Congratulations, Mrs. McCarran," Luke murmured and kissed her lips as their families cheered over the phone. "You are now officially on your honeymoon."

"So are you, Mr. McCarran, and I'm going to make sure you enjoy every moment of it," Jenny said with a light-hearted laugh.

Luke said goodbye to their families, promising to bring back lots of souvenirs then activated the camera on his phone.

"You look so happy, honey. I want to remember you just as you are in this moment," he said to Jenny as he pulled the lei over her head and motioned her to stand with her back toward a mirror-covered wall.

Jenny crossed one arm in front of her, holding her other hand close to her chin as she turned her head to one side and caught her smiling reflection in the large mirror.

"Hold it right here," Luke said and snapped the picture. "Beautiful. Just like you."

Loving him had not only made her feel beautiful on the outside but on the inside, too. She had never been so happy.

They posed for their official wedding picture and finished the ceremony by signing the wedding license.

Jenny and Luke left the little chapel carrying their shoes and strolled barefoot along the Kauai beach. The balmy evening breeze swirled gently as the ocean swooshed in and out, tickling their toes with sand and splashing their ankles with waves as warm as bathwater.

"What a magical evening," Jenny said, drawing in a deep breath of fresh air. "It's so beautiful here."

Luke slid his free arm around her waist and pulled her close. "It's magical because we're together. Every evening can be like this, no matter where we are." He stopped and pulled her close. "I love you, Jenny."

She tossed her high-heeled sandals and slid her arms around his neck. "I love—"

She never got the chance to finish, but it didn't matter. The passion in their kiss said more than words could express.

The End

A note from Denise

Thank you so much for reading ***The Encore Bride.*** If you enjoyed this story, please take a moment to post a rating or short review on Amazon. Thank you! As an indie author, ratings and/or reviews help me to reach more people who love to read sweet romance.

To be notified when a new book is available, be sure to follow me on Amazon at:

https://www.amazon.com/author/denisedevine

About the Author

Denise Devine is a USA Today bestselling author who has had a passion for books since the second grade when she discovered Little House on the Prairie by Laura Ingalls Wilder. She wrote her first book, a mystery, at age thirteen and has been writing ever since. She loves all animals, especially dogs, cats, and horses, and they often find their way into her books.

She has written twenty books, including books in the Beach Brides series, Moonshine Madness series, and West Loon Bay series. Her books have hit the Top 100 Bestseller list on Amazon and she has been listed on Amazon's Top 100 Authors.

More Books by Denise Devine

Christmas Stories

Merry Christmas, Darling

A Christmas to Remember

A Merry Little Christmas

Once Upon a Christmas

Mistletoe and Wine – *Coming Soon!*

A Very Merry Christmas - Hawaiian Holiday Series

~*~

Bride Books

The Encore Bride

Lisa – Beach Brides Series

Ava – Perfect Match Series

Della – *Coming Soon!*

~*~

Moonshine Madness Series
Historical Suspense/Romance

The Bootlegger's Wife – Book 1

Guarding the Bootlegger's Widow – Book 2

The Bootlegger's Legacy – Book 3

The Nightingale Detective Agency – Book 4 – *Coming Soon!*

~*~

West Loon Bay Series – Small Town Romance

Small Town Girl – Book 1

Brown-Eyed Girl – Book 2

Country Girl – Book 3 - *Coming Soon!*

~*~

Cozy Mystery

Unfinished Business

Dark Fortune

~ Girl Friday Cozy Series ~

Shot in the Dark – Book 1

The Accidental Detective – *Coming Soon!*

~*~

This Time Forever - an inspirational romance

Romance and Mystery Under the Northern Lights – short stories

Want more? Read the first chapter of Denise's novels on her blog at:

https://deniseannette.blogspot.com

~*~

Audiobooks Galore!

Romance, Suspense & Cozy Mystery

Check out this month's audiobooks on sale for $1.99

Many of Denise's books are available in audio! Check out Denise's website for links to each audiobook.

https://www.deniseannettedevine.com

Narrated by Lorana L. Hoopes

Monthly sales!